Ak Welsapar

THE TALE OF AYPI

NOVEL

Translated by W.M. Coulson

Glagoslav Publications

THE TALE OF AYPI

NOVEL

by Ak Welsapar

Translated by W.M. Coulson

Book created by Max Mendor

Glagoslav Publications Ltd
88-90 Hatton Garden
EC1N 8PN London
United Kingdom

www.glagoslav.com

ISBN: 978-1-78437-983-4

Contents

Ak Welsapar
(Photo by Fanny Eriksson)

About The Tale of Aypi

An impoverished pair, Araz and his wife Ay-Bebek, lie in bed arguing. Soon they must leave their village – their old village on the shores of the Caspian Sea. How very topical is this tale of the disruption of ordinary lives, of quarrels and corrupt governments. Misery abounds and there are ghosts about. Yet human determination survives.

Does this sound familiar? What is strikingly unfamiliar is that this remarkable novel, where centuries seem to roll back into desert, is the first novel ever to emerge from Turkmenistan. Having lived for a while in that beautiful, harsh land, I can swear by the brilliant atmosphere of this epic tale, and advise all readers to experience it for themselves.

Brian W. Aldiss
(Brian W. Aldiss is an English writer,
SF historian, and a critic).

The sorrowful tale of Aypi, her story with no beginning or end; spurned until only the backbone of its significance remained. Not a single person had taken any notice of the young woman's tragic end or her short life. She was lost in the darkness of centuries along with her true name – a victim of unfounded fears.

To fate: betray not these hopes!

Makhtumkuli, 18th century

1

A tanned skinny boy of ten or twelve years old leapt down from the ledge of a run-down hut propped up on stilts. Hopping like a desert mouse, he made his way through the winding streets of his village which lay just a stone's throw from the sea. His piercing cries disturbed the tangled alleys full of houses still asleep, all so like his own.

"Sturgeon! Sturgeon for sale! Sturgeon!"

Bearing a woven basket full of fish, he weaved between the shabby huts, identical like twins. Although he was moving further away, his high-pitched calls of: "Sturgeon! Sturgeon!" were still ringing all over the place.

That sound was what woke a fisherman from the sweet dawn-time sleep that he'd just found after returning home late from the sea, only to be torn away from his rest. With difficulty he rubbed both his eyes, exhausted from staring all night into the fickle autumn sea, and gloomily looked around. Not seeing his wife, he raised his voice:

"Ay-Bebek!"

No response. The thick, sandblasted fabric covering the door rustled in the wind against the old-fashioned reed walls of the house, striving to make its own meagre contribution to the perpetual rumbling of the surf. Listening to the ceaseless thundering of the waves as he had since childhood, their sound was a balm to his tired ears whenever he slept in his own home. It was irritating to be disturbed in such a crude way.

"Ay-Bebek!" he shouted again, first tilting his head, then squinting to try to keep out the pain-inflicting sunbeams coming through the porch shutters.

A dainty attractive female head with its neatly brushed hair peered out from some inner chamber.

"Calm down, I'm right here" she answered, as she straightened the black hair hanging to her knees with an ash comb. "What is it?"

"Can't that rascal be taught not to stomp around the village like that? He could just go quietly door-to-door, you know! Or has the relocation begun already?"

"Just a minute!" His wife once again disappeared into the house. She then headed out, putting on her headscarf and quietly murmuring to herself, "But the relocation is already underway, isn't it? It can't be stopped: If everyone else moves and you're the only one left, you too will have to go."

After his wife had left, the house fell silent again and the fisherman closed his eyes. Ay-Bebek's clear, pleasant voice soon rang from across the street.

"Baljan! Baljan, come here child, let me tell you something…" The boy's screeches promptly ceased.

Soon after, the woman returned, swishing aside the door tapestry as she came through. She intended to pass her husband by, yet her footsteps betrayed her. Without opening his eyes, he reached out and grabbed his young wife by her slender waist, still as graceful and lithe as a young girl's, though she was now the mother of two. Despite her resistance, he easily pulled her down towards him.

"Stop it Araz! Stop, please, you'll wake up the baby!"

"I will not."

The fisherman sprang up from his bed sheets and pressed his whole weight onto his delicate wife.

"Stop it, boy! What if the neighbours came by for a visit?" his wife scolded him, struggling to break free.

"Let 'em come! What business do they have at this hour, is their grave being dug here?"

"Just what a man like you would say — 'Neighbours?! Fine, let them come, if they want to come, why shouldn't they?'" retorted his wife, attempting to slip out of his strong eagle strong claws, gasping and burning her husband's chest with her hot breath.

"Ok, let 'em not come! I don't need them! They'll get my answer in the end!"

His wife grew increasingly angry.

"Look, boy! What did they ever do to us, for you to talk like this?"

"If they haven't done anything yet, they will, they just aren't finished yet! When the time comes, you'll see, just you wait. Lately they've been barely able to say hello to me, as if I'd stolen their catch or sunk their boats."

"No, don't slander people! They're not against us. You just take it out on everyone near you and…"

"Ok, enough! I know what they've been thinking lately, it's blatantly obvious. You know how they sniff around, waiting for the day I get caught poaching, that's when they'll be glad! However much you make excuses for their foolishness, they'll find a reason."

"You'll wear yourself out worrying. Do you think they don't want to go fishing? Who doesn't want to go out to sea? But if it's not allowed, what can simple folks do? The power's in the government's hands, what authority do we have? You'll bow down to them too in the end- you're the only one left in the village. I worry night and day for you, this whole thing is frightening me."

Araz listened patiently for a moment, then continued:

"Why shouldn't people have some power too, or greater power than them? They should, but to have power you need guts, and that means you need to open your mouth eventually. When you're no longer afraid, then you'll have the power, you see? If you just sit there and say, 'Yes sir' to any command from on high, who'll ever know that you exist? Who'll care about your situation, or listen to you? How can you be a man if you don't demand your rights?"

Ay-Bebek, maintaining her wifely caution, tried to calm her husband down.

"If you open your mouth, who knows what'll happen? What if they crack down on you? Before you know it you're separated from your children, from your hearth and home, and you'll wake up in Siberia! There's no shortage of people who were taken from the village that way. The fire's been taken out of folks' eyes, so they stay silent now".

Araz continued, paying no attention to her concerns,

"To begin the process, first people need to organize themselves. You need to learn how to think and speak as one, so that your words make an impact, otherwise it all amounts to empty threats. A lone rider raises no dust! All an individual can do is be a good example, but he can't change everything by himself alone. Man was given speech and intelligence, so why shouldn't people use these gifts when they ought to be used?"

By this point, his wife couldn't keep from bringing up her old wounds."Araz, if you hadn't been so arrogant and dropped out of college, right now you'd be the manager of some bureau in the city, wear an expensive straw hat on your head, coming and going from an air-conditioned office. Then your children and I wouldn't be baking in this terrible heat; instead we'd be living in a nice cool mansion."

"Does us going back and forth from an air conditioned mansion really solve all the world's problems?"

"No, but what are we doing here? It's all meaningless. Now that fishing has been forbidden, what's the point of staying? Wouldn't it be better to go silently where they tell us to go?"

"It's everyone's weakness that got us into this in the first place," he confirmed. "To defend your home you need both intelligence and confidence. If either of these is missing, what use is the other? Didn't our ancestors defend this coast? They did, so why shouldn't we? The legend of Aypi didn't just fall out of the sky, and this isn't the first time someone's set eyes on our folk's land and property. But in the past they defended it fearlessly. Now, we tremble."

"These are different times," said his wife sceptically.

Araz answered bitterly: "What's the difference between these days and those? If you don't defend your home, they'll try to take it from you at any time – what does the era matter?"

"We're no longer living in the ancient times," pointed out Ay-Bebek with a woman's wisdom. "Go ahead and conspire, plan, and do whatever you like, but now we've got the State, government and the laws – where can you escape from them? What's more, it isn't like people are afraid for themselves..."

Araz's voice rose: "Then who are they afraid for? Of course they're afraid for themselves; how could someone else make them into such cowards?"

Ay-Bebek attempted once more, without result, to free herself from her husband's captivity, then looked down.

"People fear for their wives and children, that's why they're cautious. But you, on the other hand, don't care about us at all."

Her husband, obviously irritated, turned over and rested his hand on his temple.

"Does someone who really cares about their family throw away their own village? Is that what you're saying? These people are just floating along on the currents, like dead fish! Their fears – it's just them wanting to save their own hides, the cowards."

Ay-Bebek, recalling that she had one or two distant relatives in the village, replied in an insulted tone, "There are no cowards here, who can you point your finger at and say 'You, coward!' Who here is a stranger to you?"

"If you fish for a living, but you won't go out to sea – then you're a coward! All these people threw away the trade passed down to them by their fathers. If you're a fisherman, go out to sea! What is there for you to do on dry land?"

Ay-Bebek didn't want to anger her husband by carrying the argument farther, so she quietly responded,

"We're all helpless…"

"Of course you're helpless: if you're afraid to organize yourself together with others, and remain in fear to speak your own mind."

"Who knows," said his wife softly, "but none of these people wish you ill."

The fisherman took a deep breath.

"You're wrong, they don't like me and won't forgive me, because I do what they can't. How could they like me? The day I'm caught, you'll see. I'm already up to my neck in fines; if they catch me again, this time it will be a metal cage. Do you think anyone will defend me? They'll forget that red sturgeon pilaf they cook at every wedding, just you wait. Why should they remember something that reflects poorly on them?"

Though she had realized she couldn't keep her husband from going out to sea, she still wouldn't stop trying to convince him at every opportunity. "I'm not saying you're wrong, but when you go out alone, the neighbours do fear that you've drowned. Do you recall that night of the big storm? I guess you spent it on Aypi's bluff, as you may remember."

"So what if I did?" her husband answered noncommittally.

"Aha! Gutly had guessed right away and came over to help us. Otherwise, would Baljan and I have been strong enough to go up on the roof and secure those heavy tarpaulins, if it had been just the two of us? No we certainly wouldn't have been! You can see what a state this household's in."

"So what if you hadn't been able to put them up? Hardship doesn't break a person – only cowardice does. Hardship makes a man's body tougher and clothes his heart with armour. I know what hardship is better than you."

"What, you think I'm saying you don't know?" she replied with hurt in her voice. "I'm just saying that our neighbours don't mean you any harm; they aren't condemning you. Their only fault is not being able to go out fishing, but don't turn that into a crime. Everyone is so tired; they've had to give up their livelihoods, and all their expectations from previous life have been shot down. Can't you understand that?"

Araz sighed, "Who isn't tired? Yet you don't see me saying I'm tired and abandoning the ways of my fathers."

"Oh Araz, Araz! You'll buckle too, like everyone else. Won't you stop doing this impossible thing, and finally give up fishing, so I can rest peacefully here at home? Will this ever happen? Can't you just be content with what makes other people happy, so we can be like everyone else? The weight of your blind courage is getting heavier and heavier, and you are failing to understand that I'm the one bearing it all!"

Araz glared at his wife. "I know you are, but whenever I take a stand, you need to stand with me. To go out to sea you need strength. Do these incompetent people have any left?

They aren't like you. Now if they do decide to go out, they aren't even able to, you know. If they go together, they're good for nothing, getting tangled up in their own nets. Recently our neighbour from around the back has been saying 'let's go roach fishing' to me-"

"Man-Weli?" his wife looked up, "See, I told you they miss the sea!"

Her husband furrowed his brow. "That's one thing I'm incapable of, to go roach fishing with them! Hand Baljan over to that group, he'll be a fitting companion for them! How can someone who hasn't gone out to sea for a year still be a fisherman? There's no difference between them and Baljan now: If they see a tiny puff of a cloud they get scared and run away. If a little gust of wind blows, they gather up their nets in a panic. If a wave no higher than a sturgeon's fin comes along – they're finished!"

"There are quite a few places where you should be wary of the sea," said his wife. "Perhaps they aren't wrong after all? Is the power of the sea something to take lightly? You always go out alone, who'll be there to help you when you need it? Too bad I am busy here with our children; otherwise I wouldn't be staying behind. Don't be like this. Can't you be content like everyone else, then we won't die hungry. Just find something to do on the side to keep yourself busy and earn a pittance."

Araz shouted angrily: "Am I a fisherman, or not? Am I some kind of herdsman? If a man can't follow his father's trade, what'll become of him? A man should be able to do what he loves! Is that too much to ask?"

"Be quiet, boy, don't trouble the neighbours, it's Bazaar day and people are sleeping; it's not like it was before, now Bazaar day is a day of rest. Yes, maybe it is as you say, but now I'm talking about something else: Nowadays no-one in this village would entrust their life to a small boat and go out fishing at night anymore. Soon there'll be no-one left here but us. By now everyone's accepted relocation. Never mind Kebe grandma, they'll relocate her too, they say they will; otherwise, if anyone stays, it'll only be her."

His wife's words affected Araz like stepping on a tapestry needle would – he didn't shout, he merely groaned. He soundlessly released his wife from his embrace, then stared at her.

"If they go, then fine, let them all go to the devil and beyond! They can go right now!! You too! I'll stay here, and I won't go anywhere even if they kill me. This is where my umbilical cord was cut; my true birthplace! And see there? Over that hill is where my ancestors are buried. How could I let myself be forced out from here? My father, and my father's father too, lie mixed with that sand, and his grandfather as well – all seven generations of my ancestors! Where would I go if I left them? This place here is my coast, my land, my waters! If the earth itself moved, I would still stay! I'd break the ribs of anyone who would try to make me, if they're tired of living!"

He turned aside and lowered his voice, gasping a little. Taking a moment to recover, he said, "As my father lay there dying, he told me: 'Don't abandon this beach or this sea. We are not shepherds; we're a settled people, fishermen. I, my father, and my father's father fished here, lived out their lives, so that you too, and your children also, might be fishermen.'" His wife's quiet sniffling interrupted the fisherman's sad voice, but Araz resumed after a momentary pause. "This coast is the inheritance my father left me. If I washed my hands of it, I'd be nothing, understand? Nothing! Now though, I have some honour. At least it's right in front of me. While I live on my own coast and land, in my own home, I'm a man. So let those folks go where they may; I have no other place to go. I will stay."

Sensing his wife's tears, silent as always, he turned to her, and took her back into his arms. With his strong hands he accurately wiped the tears from her wet cheeks.

"Araz, how will this all end?" she asked quietly. "If only I knew everything would be all right, then I could endure it all, but I'm terrified, I feel some misfortune coming; Last night I was scared that you wouldn't return, and I've had nightmares again. Lately as soon as my eyelids shut, the nightmares come."

The fisherman hugged his wife reassuringly, pressing her in against his chest, which still smelled of the brackish waters.

"You'll have fewer bad dreams. Whenever I'm late, remember I'll come back eventually. It's always been that way, and it always will be. Anyway, 'the pitcher can only sink in water, not on dry land.'"

With this, he brought his wife closer to himself with a different sort of force. In his powerful arms, she became eclipsed like the moon behind the edge of a cloud, until only her black hair on the pillow remained seen. Her husband's sun-blackened, sea-beaten shoulders turned to salt on her warm lips and tongue.

2

According to legend, some 300 years ago a group of strange men from unknown lands came ashore on this beach. The unexpected guests had dropped anchor without encountering any sort of welcome until a young woman, Aypi, who often gathered beautiful stones from the beach, came across the newcomers by chance. Not being particularly timid, she spoke with them, and it seems they were inquisitive folk, since their talk went on for some time. When they did at last part, the strangers gave the woman a stunning ruby necklace. The thing shone with such an arresting sanguine glow that Aypi was tempted to immediately put it on, and as soon as she re-entered the village, everyone took note of the remarkable trinket.

Indeed, the necklace from across the seas dazzled all who crossed her path. She strutted haughtily through the winding streets of ramshackle stilt-propped huts, until there wasn't a woman or girl left in the village who didn't envy her.

As she passed by one young wife's door, the woman grabbed her arm. "Come on Aypi, tell me," she asked suspiciously, "where'd you get that fine piece?"

"'Where'd you get it?'" smirked Aypi. "That's what they say to a thief, girl! Some foreigners I saw down on the beach gave this to me."

The other woman narrowed her eyes and asked insinuatingly: "They got enticed by your looks, did they?" spearing a meaningful look at the crowd of women gathered around.

"Oh no, girl," cooed Aypi, who had always been proud of her beauty. "It's not that at all, don't be silly."

"Strange... so why'd they give you that, huh? 'Cuz a your Persian-like name?" she quipped, as the circle of women grew ever tighter around them.

"Speak up quick, girl, why'd they give ya that? Stop wasting our time, and spill the beans!"

Aypi gave them a sugary smile. "I told them about our life, our village and our chiefs, and when I showed 'em how our men catch fish, they laughed and laughed."

Now the women gaped even more.

"They gave you such a thing for that nonsense? Any of us could have told them the same, if they'd only asked!"

"I told them about the coast here, and listed all the villages. Not one of you know better'n me how many people are in each village!"

This made their stomachs knot: Look at that smug tramp, and see what luck she'd had! All the men's eyes were on her, as it was, and now she had that ruby necklace!

Only one sighing wreck of a crone remained aloof from the crowd, puckering her leathery face.

She wiggled her chin, pursed her lips, then, muttering and grumbling, she made her way towards Aypi, even pushing aside some of the onlookers. "Stand back, it's none of your business!" the young women scolded her, bewitched by the ruby. The grandmother was forced to wait until things calmed down, and her toothless but carefully weighed-out words would be heard by all.

"May yer eyes cloud over, hrmph," said the crone, waving her petrified clot of a fist. "You'll bring calamity down on us all! Draw a disaster! 'Round your neck the outsiders didn't hang that cursed necklace for nothing, no, they wouldn't have!

May your nipples crack, yes crack! You come back here and you've betrayed all we've got, you mug of mugs, hmmph... you told everything, there'll be no plenty on these shores no more, you've snowed a blizzard on our happiness, a blizzard!"

The old woman wandered off, muttering, "Would that yer eyes cloud over, ye bitch! Likely you've gotten us all murdered, yes, murdered!"

She was of the same age as the Flood and had seen everything there was to see, so fear began creeping into the listeners' hearts as they heard her curses. The women immediately dispersed, and left Aypi standing dumbfounded and alone in the middle of the street. The words from the crone's mouth, "She's snowed a blizzard on our happiness, a blizzard!" echoed in their ears as they fled.

In the evening the town's whitebeards held a meeting. As he was leaving their council, Dadeli, the village's best man and Aypi's husband, dragged like an anchor the weight of the sentence dealt out to his darling wife. The elders' words rang in his ears: "What she said to the strangers doesn't concern us. What scares us is that she had dealings with them at all. She has no place among us."

After the door had shut behind Dadeli, one of the old councilmen abruptly spoke out what had been in everyone's hearts without even knowing it:

"Well let's hope it's for the best!" he lamented. "She tortured everybody with her beauty. Enough! Out of sight, out of mind!"

The next day, before the town had begun to stir, on the pretence of showing her a certain islet, her husband sailed out to sea with her.

"Wear your best clothes," he had said, "and put on that ruby necklace too, look how it suits you!" They had left the village before sunrise. As they got on the boat, Aypi could already sense the tension, but only after they had arrived and climbed up the lonely peak did she take a look into her husband's frozen eyes and know her fate. In the final moments, she broke away from him in an attempt to flee, but Dadeli's burly arms encircled her. From the cliff's very pinnacle he pushed her down into the frothing swell. The strange necklace's weight gave her no chance to swim, but dragged her down, twisting, into the depths of the briny waters.

Ever since, the people on the coast were haunted by the fear that those uninvited guests would return someday, bearing not gifts, but weapons.

3

Sometime in the early afternoon, a group of local men gathered on the beach beside an old scuttled sailboat that had been there since their grandfathers' time. They would roll their cigarettes and endlessly puff on bitter tobacco, their faces wrinkled by old sorrows.

The impending irreparable calamity of recent years was now upon them: they'd been ordered to immediately relocate to the city post, where new homes made of concrete awaited them. Some of them had already moved and began acclimatizing to the new location and lifestyle. Those who remained, still lived with a glimmer of hope, however slim, that perhaps this time, like several years before, the powers above would relent. For that reason, the stragglers hemmed and hawed and seemed in no rush.

Actually, the whole affair had begun with pleasant and even joyful news. Several years ago, a group of medical scientists conducting an investigation in the area had declared, "The whole coast is simply a natural wonder!" As they further explained, "the continuous abrasive force of the waves against the coastal shelf creates elevated levels of ionization in the atmosphere. In such conditions, people suffering from illnesses whose cases have been deemed hopeless could make full recoveries. If, for example, you were to open a sanatorium for asthmatics and people with other respiratory diseases, this stretch of coast would be simply invaluable!"

Following this, a stream of renowned and reputable administrators poured in from the capital to the secluded village, where previously, for months and even years at a time, no stranger would set foot. The scientists brought along with them every kind of instrument, conducted in-depth examinations of local conditions, debated incessantly, and concocted a number of schemes.

As the village fishermen observed all this commotion, at first their heads swelled with pride. Look here, if they hadn't been living for generations in such a health-giving, astounding location!

In no time at all, the strangers began to transport construction materials to the site. A line of monstrous vehicles rolled in bearing a number of wheeled wooden houses, in which it was confirmed the construction workers would reside. The village children immediately gathered around them, knocking and poking the trailers to test the vehicles' strength against their own, and marvelled at the smell of new paint as they sniffed in the scents of the trailers. A few of the smallest toddlers had even licked the wheeled houses out of curiosity. The older boys soon clambered up onto the roofs of the trailers and spent hours there gazing at the sea, arguing about nothing at all and dreaming until dark, as boys always will. As they understood it, this coast would quickly become a fine place and things would pick up considerably. If hunger and darkness hadn't chased them off the rooftops of these dwellings, they would be ready to stay night and day up there, speculating about such matters.

The joy of both boys and men was short-lived. At first they had congratulated themselves, "If they build this sanatorium here, then they'll build us nice new brick houses." Soon though a disturbing thought arose – "If they build it, what will become of our village?" This negative aspect only then became clear, and soon the matter was resolved decisively and contrary to the hopes of the fishermen: The village had no future, fishing was now forbidden, and never mind all those who had always done this, let them find new jobs in the city. The fishermen's elation had been extinguished with a single breath only to be replaced with grief and panic: What should they do? Whitherto should they run? Whom should they entreat, and from what quarter could they expect help?

Then, without warning, construction ceased of its own accord, and the fishermen found themselves free for a year. The trailers vanished. Due to poor planning, funds had apparently run out. Several months later however, the process began all over again. As it turned out, this time everything was much more serious: an order came that everyone must be deported from the area, without causing any interruption to the ongoing work.

Half a century ago these old fishermen had rowed all the way to the Russian capital just to make a name for themselves. Then the times had changed, and, like broken toys, the men now sat down in the shadows of this rotten ancient sailboat just beside those same wasted dinghies. At first no one made a sound because unsurprisingly they'd already discussed all their options. It was clear enough. Without any new suggestions to be made, what could they possibly discuss? No one wanted to start anything, so they sat, each minding his own business. Finally, Nur Tagan, an elder fisherman, stepped forward and launched into a tirade expressing his long-held opinions:

"Yes, indeed, men, my guess is as good as any, and I say from now on we won't be able to change a thing. There are things we can do, and things we can't. We'll be moving soon, and our ancestors' lands will slip through our fingers, but what can we do? Tomorrow I might go to the city and see my new house there for myself. If you want to come along with me, hop onto the mail truck." After a few moments of reflection, he added "Don't look so sad. Honestly, most of our children have already been there for a while, let's not be stubborn.

After that, a bad-tempered discussion sprang into life. No one seemed to get much consolation from Nur Tagan's opinion, though his fellow long-beard Mered Badaly did take his side because of his two boys, both of whom had already been living in the city. They had studied or whatnot there, taken up city work, and eventually dropped anchor. The elder, Kerim, was married, and the younger, Kerem, had no desire to return to the village.

"Hrrm! Ahem!" coughed Mered Badaly, clearing his throat as a preface to his speech: "You've got it right, long-beard. We ought to live near our children. I stayed up all night thinking about it, and spent all the evening pondering it too. How couldn't I? Come on; speak up, which of you hasn't been bashing your head against the wall over this? I have just one thought: without us, in the city I mean, won't our grandchildren become complete strangers in no time at all? Already we can't understand our own children when they talk, so you can imagine for yourself how it will be with the grandkids. They'll be lost, there's no denying it."

"Now, there's a reason I say this, men. I make conclusions based on what's in front of me. Much as they boast, if we're not around, their affairs won't be so respectable, is what I say. You can see something particularly sheepish written across their faces. Last time the boys visited, the old lady and I couldn't believe their behaviour. We didn't understand why they sulked so, good heavens if they had even said a word to us! Yes sir, I asked myself if they hadn't forgotten how to talk! It's like they didn't come from the city but the deepest desert. They brood without setting their eyes on the people 'round them, and don't utter a single word. Yes indeed, if you've got nothing better to do, come see it for yourselves!"

My older boy Kerim, when I asked him "Son, why don't you ever say a word from morning to night, like your mouth's full of water?" he said "Father, We're focused on our inner lives." How am I to understand this "inner life" of theirs? So I told him, "Listen boy, perhaps it's fun for you to live inside yourself, and you don't need anyone else to talk to, but we sure do. If you clam up, who will us old folks, talk to? Who can we discuss things with? If you won't talk with us, and then someday if your children – our grandchildren – won't talk to you, what'll be the end of all this?" And so he answers "Everyone must act according to their 'Tellekt."

Tall Hodja, confused, raised himself a little:

"What did you say, old man?"

"T-E-L-L-E-K-T" said Mered Badaly, spelling it out especially for him. "That's what he said, how am I supposed to know what he means?"

A younger fisherman in a straw hat couldn't stop himself from chuckling as he corrected his elder – "It wasn't 'Intellect' by any chance, was it, uncle Mered Badaly?"

"Ah yes, so it was, he said something or other like that, may well be so. Will you look at the words these people come up with! If you try to repeat it your tongue'll break. Really, when they speak in this way, it's no easy thing for the likes of us to understand. How about that, those words coming from their mouths! Anyway, is that a sign of intelligence? These folks, I don't reckon they're all that intelligent; in fact it's probably all a result of soft-headedness."

"Basically, I'm saying that all of these things result from them not being around us, what else could it be? It's clear they're having a fine time of it in the city without us! We old folks are obviously needed there. And how much! Otherwise the traditions of our ancestors will slip away into the sands, and our children will lose their native language. How else can they be brought up with education and learning, and, as it were, humanity? Look here, we let them fly too early from the nest, or we wouldn't now be facing this kind of trouble. We weren't able to teach them one third of what we'd learnt from our old folks, that blame's on us. Television and books might not be teaching them anything bad, but they can't get the example they were meant to take from us, from those other things, and that's a fact. Sooner or later we've got to do the hard work ourselves, because no one else can."

"I couldn't have said it better myself!" responded Hodja, standing up. "I've seen this television thing of theirs! Isn't it a wonder! A spectacle, alright! Whatever you want to see, there it is: on a summer's day you can see snow – if it pleases ye! And in the winter you can see scorching heat, it has that too. Finer than you can imagine! Although you can't touch anything with your hand, there's great crowds inside it: jumping, dancing and even walking on their heads. One sings, one plays an instrument, one swallows fire and another kills you with laughter – whatever you like! I wouldn't say it's just interesting; it's impossible to stop watching. If you kneel down before it, so long as those dancers keep dancing, you'll sit there heedless of all your cares and duties."

"But whatever you might say, I never saw this place on that television. I came back from the city without learning we existed at all. If you think that's nothing, well, the people who watch television also listen to it and most of the ones who speak on it are young people themselves. As long as I have watched it, I've never seen seasoned wise old folks giving advice to youngsters and I certainly didn't see any well-behaved child pouring water from a pitcher onto his grandfather's hands. Why is this? I thought to myself, is this a case of "Yesterday's sparrow teaching today's sparrow how to tweet?" It's a matter of training them, see? So if you can go after them, then go, by all means! But we don't benefit them at all if we just keep sitting on this lifeless coast here, doing nothing."

"That's what I'm saying too," agreed Mered Badaly. "Moving to the city quickly is the best thing we can do; let's be near our grandchildren, perhaps it will do them some good. They can't develop without us and what's more, without us they won't know themselves – no knowledge at all of their elders. What can you expect from children who grow up in such a way? They'll probably make all kinds of mistakes we can't even imagine, because big and small they're always in front of that television. They take their lessons from it and that's why their behaviour is going way off. Let's say that box shows some house burning in the far corner of the earth – they'll gasp in horror and pity the people burning inside, but they have no idea about their own neighbour lying sick in bed for however many months; they have nothing to do with him, though he's living right there next to them!"

Gutly, the young fisherman, who had taken correspondence courses from the institute and went to the city every now and then, straightened his straw hat. "Walls of iron and concrete interfere even with radio waves and they're a definite obstacle to emotional waves."

"What? You want to make a joke of this?" Hodja grumbled. "You've forgotten that people are supposed to be compassionate towards each other, otherwise what's the difference between us and animals? Wearing clothes? You can always put clothes on a horse or a dog for that matter!"

Mered Badaly continued, despite the interruptions, summarising briefly: "Well then, that's what this 'inner life' of theirs means."

Hodja had another question: "Old friend, we've heard of the 'next life,' and we're living 'this life' right now, but really, what kind of life is their 'inner life?' Where is it actually? Wouldn't it be a bit cramped?"

Gutly had the answer before Mered Badaly could respond. A pleasant smile appeared on his round face to show that, as usual, he had an especially choice remark: "Hodja, their "inner life" is located right between 'this life' and 'the next life!'"

The men all laughed at the joke, and then they began to make fun of the village laughingstocks. "What's more beautiful," one asked at Pirim's expense, "a bottle of vodka, or a woman? Which one is hotter, and which one is quieter?" For a while they forgot all about relocation. How can you escape worry though, especially if your worry is justified?

4

A few days later, when they next gathered on the same spot, the old men were finally compelled to discuss with each other what they had always avoided mentioning: namely when they would relocate. Like it or not, this had to be resolved, before the problem forced its own resolution. Naturally, after quite a bit of beating around the bush, the council got underway. Hodja spoke his mind first:

"'Shipmates share their soul' they say, and if we've gotta go, let's not drift off one by one, but let's pick a day and ship out together."

Everyone looked away and shuffled uneasily, as if a bright light was shone at them in the dark.

"Seems Kebe grandma finally agreed," remarked fat Rejeb, glancing around and sharing the news he'd heard from his wife at noon. "If she has seen the house set aside for her, said 'ok' and returned, it couldn't be that bad."

"Is there anything else to say?" confirmed one old man. "Kebe grandma was dead-set against leaving. She's our poor widow; even if we flew to the moon we couldn't leave her behind."

Bally halfhand sighed, "What a pity, she never lost hope for Gadam." He ran his maimed hand across his face in a habitual gesture. Two fingers from his right hand he'd left behind in the middle of Europe at the end of the Second World War, and no matter how much people respected him and called him 'Bally father' to his face, behind his back they would refer to him as 'halfhand'. Though he knew this nickname, he took no offence from his comrades, just saying, "If you escape from a bloody fight like that with just fingers missing, you should count yourself lucky, I certainly did."

This man Bally seemed to have also left behind all capacity for anger on that battlefield, and didn't think anything in life was worth getting angry over. Whenever any person began to antagonize him, he'd just say, "Cut it out!" then went on his way. He never argued or squabbled with anyone. Though he wasn't a relative, he was one of the villagers who took daily care of old Kebe, and he was well acquainted with her situation. "A pity alright, she's still waiting for her husband. She believes he'll come, and will until she sees his body. When a storm comes she doesn't sleep, just wanders along the beach thinking that since he was lost in a storm, he'll come back in a storm. But the water didn't give up his body and it won't give itself up, so what good will praying do?"

Rejeb looked at the sea and remarked "Let me see, since the squall got Gadam it's been 20 years or so at least, probably even more."

"That's right" Bally affirmed. "But as the years pass, our widow Kebe seems to hope even more that he'll return. As long as she's near the coast, her soul finds comfort. She doesn't fit in her own land, makes you wonder how she'll pass her days in the city? Would she ever stop grieving here, we wondered? Instead the old woman will fade away crying in a strange new place. But what can be done? Everyone has their lot wherever you go with it, as fate decrees."

Rejeb regarded the old veteran a moment, and said: "That's true with fate, but men have other enemies besides destiny, Bally. The State isn't far behind fate – whatever you do have – they're ready to take it away."

"Ha, the government is this era's fate, and there's no denying it", confirmed Man-Weli bitterly.

Gutly grasped his hat in his hand as though he were going to crush it. "The old folks here didn't live in fear of destiny," he cried out, "it's said they stood fast when it challenged them."

"History repeats itself" the village's oldest man, Nur Tagan said, with a gloomy smile. "At least, if you fail to protect your rights either fate will take them away or someone else will."

"Nur Tagan, It's easy to fight with this destiny thing – it's totally insubstantial, so go ahead and swing away at it with your sword. The State's a different matter. It exists all right! Go out and challenge it – you'll see what happens."

Gutly spoke with the phrases of books he had read: "For a person to defend their rights is beneficial to everyone: themselves, the state, and perhaps even to fate."

Bally-halfhand brought the men's discussion back down to earth. "That's if people aren't weak. If they are, then they lose their way; just like our old Kebe wanting some favour from Aypi. I saw the poor wretch praying to her, "If my lost man is at the bottom of the sea, send me a word."

Mered Badaly was surprised. "What help can Aypi give to fishermen?" he asked pointedly. "When folk go out to sea they don't speak the doomed woman's name, they say it's bad luck – an evil spirit. Who hopes for good news from her? In all our years we've never seen nor heard of anyone kneeling to her. What help can one unlucky wretch give to another?"

"You'll see soon enough," said Man-Weli, furrowing his grizzled eyebrows, "that poor soul's sins are no greater than anyone else's, and folk shouldn't speak so ill of that one. It won't make them happy, and no good will come of it. If a gift is given, is there anyone who would turn it down? Who of you would?"

"Are you saying that these folks here killed her, like?" said Bally, cupping his face with his right hand.

"What do you mean 'like?' Hodja said, though he wanted to end the discussion.

"I'm saying, it's very hard to refuse a gift, whoever you are."

"If you don't refuse what needs to be refused, it's a disgrace, how about that?" asked Mered Badaly. "Basically good or bad, guilty or innocent, there's no shame in being cautious of the same ghost that everyone else is careful of. I never heard of anyone who heeded Aypi and met with any luck, as you well know. She's the embodiment of trouble."

Man-Weli didn't want to sit there and bicker with his elder, so he mused philosophically: "This could be for other reasons: People need villains, and if they don't find one, they'll make an enemy out of one of their own eyes. That's how it is today and always has been; in Aypi's day it was probably the same, could it have been any different?"

"That's right!" agreed Gutly. "People have a very peculiar characteristic: They slander someone or other for their own fears, then they'll make an enemy of them. Aypi – our fear, and our fear of each other! She's an imaginary person, you see. There's no historical person behind the legend, it's just an empty fable."

Mered Badaly burst out angrily: "Listen boy! Why do you think people say, 'Where there's smoke, there's fire?' If it's been passed down from generation to generation, who are you to say it's completely false? It must have happened – the necklace, and the strange warriors too. What do you think an enemy does? Does he have to jump out and say 'boo!' when he arrives? If he comes and attacks you, that's an enemy. Didn't we see that for ourselves in the war? Who would say those weren't real enemies? You're making everything out to be so fine and dandy!"

"Okay there, old friend, let the past be the past. Don't bring that all up again and bully the youngsters," said Hodja, trying to steer the flow of the discussion towards another course.

"I'm not bullying the youngsters, I'm just telling them things they should know," demurred Mered Badaly.

"I think they've learned their lesson. They don't need to be too smart to understand a ghost story, they just need a good ear," said Bally, staring at the sky and reflecting a moment. The weather was changing and the sight of scattered clouds over the sea reminded him of one reckless fisherman's absence from their ranks. "Say, has anyone heard from Araz lately? How long will he bear a grudge?"

"We don't know where he is or what he's up to, maybe the young men know," said Nur Tagan, glancing over.

None could answer to the question though. "If he hasn't shown himself," complained tall Hodja, "how can these people have seen him?"

"He's avoiding us, that's for certain," replied Nur Tagan, "but one day he'll have to relocate too. If he's offended by us, well, we aren't offended by him. It's just common decency for us to tell him we're relocating. If we share what's on our mind with him, we'd find out his thoughts."

"Why doesn't he speak to us at all?" said Rejeb accusingly. "However things stand, he shouldn't isolate himself from everyone, we wish him no harm."

"He came to me one day," admitted Gutly.

"Really? What did he say?" Everyone suddenly became interested. "What's he up to? Is he getting ready to relocate? Will he go or not?"

Gutly shook his head. "No, he still just says 'I won't.' And he begged me not to either. 'Let us all stay' he said. 'Tomorrow if they decide to build something else in this new place of yours, will you leave that too? If you carry on this way, one of these days you'll end up in Siberia. If just one person in this village would understand that, we wouldn't have to relocate. It ought to be you, you studied in the capital,' he pleaded with me."

"There's truth in what he says, but we're not at fault, who here is relocating voluntarily?" complained Rejeb. "If it were really so essential, couldn't they have built the spa a few kilometres down from here? It has to be built exactly here? Or could they not give us space for a new village a little way away! This is all nonsense. Without even asking, they're taking our homes from us!"

"Ah, 'taking' you say," said Gutly, adjusting his straw hat, "Don't speak imprecisely: Actually, they've already taken them. What's more, they've already drawn a dotted line around us."

"What are you on about?" Hodja asked Rejeb. "Listen friend, we've asked the commission that came here together. They said it very clearly, that is to say, the sanatorium has to be built right here supposedly. 'No can do, you must relocate, and what's more, you're forbidden to fish, so what difference does it matter where you live?' That's what they said."

"Anyway," lamented Nur Tagan, it seems we were ignorant as far as fish and men were concerned." We've been so conceited and proud and now the ones taking everything from us don't even know who we are. First they've taken our ancestors' profession from us, and now they'll take our ancestors' land and destroy our homes. Is there anything that can be done, or isn't there? I know at any rate that they won't put us together with the asthmatics. If the factory workers who inhaled poison with every breath take a treatment here they'll recover right away. To provide relief for the sick, well, that's fine. It's not right to be an obstacle to good works, is it? We're healthy people and we'll make a new life in the city. 'Need cuts down the poplar,' turns out to be true in this case, but whether it was really need, or a needless affair, God only knows."

The men sat silently listening to the thundering sea lullaby. They were suspended between two worlds; they'd have to give up the coast and their livelihoods forever. How would they pass the days to come? The relocation drew near, and the impending loss sank deeper into their souls. They understood better than ever that they were coast men and their fondness for the sea grew ever stronger. They had been raised decently by their parents and since childhood brought up with the strength of the sea. Those crashing waves had soothed them to sleep while they were still in the bellies of their mothers, and filled their ears with song. They woke also to the sea's sweet murmur and felt a deep, professed love to it. As their parting neared, this feeling only grew stronger. Though they were loath to admit it to each other, or even themselves, it was in these moments that Araz's words rang in their hearts, and in this matter they knew that they were silent comrades, in mind and spirit, of that rebellious fisherman. Perhaps, if they, like Araz, did not heed the decree, and if they could refuse the relocation as one, everything would be different. Truly, they were caught in between two worlds!

Gutly walked over to the water's edge and turned to the men leaning against the ship. "All our ancestors fished for a living. No one knows better than we do when to fish, and for which fish. It's mind-boggling to think that all our knowledge has become useless."

"Yes, useless! Of course they'll find some machine to replace us, and that's that!" answered Man-Weli. "It will know all those things better than we do. Robots are more hardworking than humans and more humane too. They can't be as greedy as people: If you tell them to fish, they'll fish, if you tell them to carry something, they'll carry it. There's black greed in men though, they can't watch over their own affairs, and they won't stand where they ought to."

"If a robot is made to be greedy, then what?" mocked Gutly. "There'll be greedy robots after all! Don't tell me it's impossible."

Man-Weli stood his ground. He picked up a small pile of sand in his strong hands, poured it from one palm to another, slowly at first, then scratched at a childhood wound on his right cheek, and finally slapped his hand on his knee. "Know what? Whatever you say, robots will never harm the world the way people have, because robots were created only for specific tasks, not for life in general."

Gutly grabbed his hat by the brim and laughed. "Hold it, buddy! Some say that robots will make themselves some day. Who's to say what manner of offspring they'll produce?"

The older men, abashed as the discussion ventured again into areas unknown to them, narrowed their eyes.

"Even if these machines you're talking about are ever able to harvest fish on this coast, they'll never do it like men!" insisted Nur Tagan, bringing the daydreaming men back down to earth. "Once I took a fish out of my net and looked into its eyes. I threw her back into the sea, because I saw grief in those eyes. Let's see your machines look into a fish's eye and realise that it's about to drop roe! No, that contraption will just think it's a fat fish. What do you say to that? Ah, my boys, my boys! I have nothing to say about your wits. Whatever must be, must be; you're all more educated than us, so of course, you must know more than us. The opportunities you had to learn were much different too, at your age we went for weeks without a piece of bread. All grain went to horses and we went by foot. There was war after war; it was desperate times in general, but what can be said? Obviously, this is a different age with its different ways! But there's one thing I don't understand. I don't see you getting any benefit from this education of yours. You're no different from us in the way you conduct yourself, and you've no abundance of accomplishments. It's worse than in our case actually. You're kind of spineless: if someone is pushing you, if you don't mind me saying so, you don't ask why they're doing it, or even turn around to look, you just keep letting yourself get packed into a hole, I'd say. Bless me, you brilliant fellows! For all your reading and studying, your life is still more or less ours. That is to say, whatever you've read has no connection with real life, it seems!" concluded the old man, coming to a pause. He blew some air into his wooden pipe, then cleaned the ash out of it and knocked his bowl against his knee before continuing.

"How long will the laws meant for us, for this very place," and here he kicked the ground demonstratively, "we're sitting on now, be made in places we've never seen? How long will they be made by the hands of others, not by people who know this land's traditions? Someone who has no respect for this place is only going to make annoying, oppressive laws. If I'm not mistaken, they just make them to piss people off, don't they? You're of the same age as these strange experts, and your knowledge isn't less than theirs, but you can't do anything, and you have no power at all. Your education and your knowledge, don't do anything, neither for you nor the rest of us: Whatever you learned stayed in the place you learned it. All you are is 'angels without any miracles'."

He finally lit his pipe and then continued. "We're old men now, it's obvious. Most of us are gone and few remain. That's justice anyway: You ate, you lived, you saw good and evil, you suffered what you had to suffer, and you had your children. Then, all at once and before you know it, you're sent on your way. As for you lot though, this is what I'm trying to say: It's better to be ignorant and useful than learned and useless. There, take that on board!"

The old fisherman fell silent.

Gutly lay down on the clean sand and stared at the sky. In the heavens, just as on earth, rippled an endless, edgeless blue sea: a bottle-blue sea. The slowly gathering clouds looked to him like paradise isles on the celestial sea, which never ceased moving towards some dreamy, far-off coast. How he wished he could abandon all his terrestrial cares to live on one of those islands!

The young man's eyes measured the width and breadth of the sky-sea for a long while. He relaxed, and his mind wandered until it began to drift from the earth. He perceived the sandy beach swaying slowly, and his surroundings gradually turning to mist.

5

The winter passed, then spring came. If you saw the blooming flowers on the dunes, they would lift your spirits. Spring's beauty faded in this area as quickly as a flower petal. The season came and carpeted the desert with red, but before your eyes could take it in, it was gone. See? At high noon, the sun is already sending people to look for their shadows. As far as Araz was concerned though, it had at least gotten rid of the winter fogs.

No one spoke more than necessary with him, nor did he say much to them. Though they shared a village, they were on different continents, between which a crack in the earth had opened, and which continued to widen so that crossing from one side to the other was no longer a simple thing, and if you risked the first step, there was no guarantee of safety.

Araz himself gave no little care to the crevasse's waxing breadth and depth. These people were his community and besides their ineptitude and tractability, what were their sins? Was it all in his mind? Perhaps Ay-Bebek was right, they meant no harm. Maybe they were not really cowards, but only timid? Whom had caution ever hurt? Might not caution benefit him as well?

"No!" he would say, arguing with himself. "There's a league between caution and concession." These folks are just weak. Worst of all, they're the majority now, so they can make out their weakness as bravery if they need to. If you're the majority, why wouldn't you?"

Araz was the last, so his truth looked false. If they'd done as he said, they'd have organized themselves and refused to relocate; they ought to show some healthy opposition to this process. There's no way they would deploy troops to relocate the villagers. Would they? If the troops did come, fine, shouldn't you at least clench your fist and stand up to them? Then they'd see who had fists. If they had to relocate, they could hold on to the bitter end until nothing else was left, and only then be kicked out. These people though, if just two straw-hatted magnates appeared, they'd pile up their property and sit smugly atop it like chickens, ready to flee soon as you said, "shoo!"

Rumour had it that Mered Badaly's second son had found himself a bride in the city and one with an influential father at that, who'd travel to Moscow four or five times a year. After the marriage had been arranged, if he'd wavered before, Mered Badaly'd now become cringing and compliant, eager to avoid damaging this illustrious in-law's reputation, hadn't he? If you look closely, you will see that everyone in this life has some pitiful little personal advantage that they're chasing after, rather than the community's best. Maybe you would want to respond, 'No, I won't admit to this,' but if you look closely, you'll be disappointed. Should you try to find some big reason behind it, you'd find only little things. If the villagers had anything real to gain by giving up the village, that would be something he could understand, but it was just their own personal gain! That's what infuriated him – how could these personal benefits be worth condemning your whole community?

Araz vowed to himself that he would go to the boy's wedding, sit next to them all and talk nicely. He didn't want to crash the party, but just have a talk with his neighbours.

After the TV and radio had joyfully proclaimed that the fishermen were voluntarily giving up their village for the asthma sanatorium, and after all this had been explained to the village elders, their relocation wouldn't be delayed much longer. There was no way they would send troops to the village, Araz knew well; who would do such a thing? After all, the current efforts were quite enough to dispirit the villagers: The once weekly food deliveries had reduced to every other week, and when water from the boreholes ran out, they were advised to drink spring water instead, but the previously regular monthly ferry from Baku that would bring the spring water to fill the wells had been discontinued this year. In addition, the bus route that went to the city three times weekly came just once now, and the mail was late too. There it was if you needed it, the marvel of "voluntary" undertakings.

All this incensed Araz, but the spinelessness of his comrades infuriated him most of all. Yet, there was nothing to be done but stifle his rage, grumbling his way through town; only when he was with the sea, his only confidant, did peace come.

With nothing else left to do, the village was busy preparing to celebrate the final wedding that would ever be held there. The day hadn't been quite set, but whenever people met, Kerem's cosmopolitan bride and her very prominent father were the talk of the town. The girl was beautiful, educated, and wealthy, they said, and her father was rich, with one foot in the capital. Of course, people made a fulltime occupation of clacking their tongues and repeating nonsense they heard from each other, whereas the blatant theft of their entire life didn't seem to be on their mind at all.

Araz was baffled. Someone gets married, and everyone else makes a fuss about it. What kind of a world is this! Anyway, however beautiful that girl is, what good does it do? Let's say she were cross-eyed, if Badaly's son loved her, then what difference is it to you all? Obviously she hadn't turned out cross eyed – she was beautiful, and her father was a bigshot, but would this do a speck of good in terms of keeping their village? "Nope," Araz quickly answered, but then corrected himself: "Ah, but it will make a difference; this connection will actually harm the village, since it "benefits" this future relative if Mered Badaly obediently joins the refugees.

Mered Badaly's actions were transparent enough, but what could be said for the others? At this point it resembled a wounded man using the last of his strength to smile before passing away. They were weeping on the inside only to display fake happiness on the outside. Well, they couldn't convince Araz, or even themselves, like that. So whom could they convince? Maybe they had told themselves that if they persuaded the suits and ties that they were happy, the ones who were tearing away their forefathers' land from them, they wouldn't feel bad about themselves, or consider themselves guilty? Did they think that their hearts would suddenly burst if they felt bad? What a disgrace.

After a moment, he didn't consider his musings so impractical. If Mered Badaly's new in-law was so important, it was probable that some of the paper shufflers responsible for the village's destruction might be present. Yes, they'd make an appearance for sure. Among such people ass-kissing and petty ambition was the rule, so if Mered Badaly's in-law had the loftier position, the others would surely flock here.

The thought of the contrived, sham gathering filled him with dread. How could he mingle with the fake faces, and how could he stand a whole day of their plastic smiles? Wouldn't it be a terrible bore? Ay-Bebek, terrified that he would create a scene at the wedding, begged him to behave normally and leave everyone alone. Though she had been previously, now she wasn't even opposed to him going fishing that day. He felt sorry for his helpless wife and naturally he would try to restrain himself. If he couldn't though, if they insulted him for example, then they'd see for themselves how it would end.

6

After centuries at the bottom of the sea, Aypi's troubled spirit stirred. Her ghost swam up through the strata of brine and into the dusk. The impending relocation had affected even the village ghost.

Rather than ranging far, she remained near the smouldering ashes of the life that was once dear to her, whirling around the village all night. Throwing aside the weight of the centuries, she coursed through the open air, and without bodily form to obstruct her, she was as free as the wind to sneak through any aperture she desired, only to leave again just as freely. For a time she flew through the top of one house, left through the door, then entered through the door of another house, and then out again through the roof.

Though she flitted around them all night, the appearance of the village, and the objects within the homes did little to catch her eye. She stopped a moment to look at the novel appliances, but these too failed to amaze her. At first, the cold chests with food inside drew her attention especially. When she scrutinized their insides however, she lost interest; the wheezing boxes were mostly empty. They may not have had these chilling boxes in her day, but at least there had been plenty of fresh fruit! It would make sense if they were meant for storing cold water, which you could then drink and be satisfied with less food. Aside from the matter of produce, the lack of fresh fish, or at least dried and salted fish, amazed the ghost. Had they grown too lazy even to fish? How did they make their living, and why were there fish in only one or two homes? Where were the sturdy canoes, skiffs, and boats that should be lying on the beach, lapped by the waves? Had some been lost, that they now be so few? What of the men who went out to sea from dawn until dusk, where were they? Where was the wild game and the sugar sweets that women and children loved so much? It looked like the village had been completely cut off from the outside world. Had its inhabitants taken fright and isolated themselves? If so, how did these fishless fishermen spend their days?

Naturally, there were other things in the houses that Aypi did not recognize or even comprehend the nature of. In a few, she found a box with a square glass face, but it was dark when she took the cover off. She didn't understand what it was, and she supposed the fishermen didn't understand either – it was probably just some time-waster and general lure of their attentions.

As she wandered into some of the wealthier homes, she had to admit that there was prosperity. Yes, there were things here in quantities that couldn't compare with her own age; and yet, she didn't discern any particular happiness on the inhabitants' faces. If it had been there, she would have seen that on their sleeping faces instead of unease and discomfort. Just then, the sleeper she had been observing made an anguished sound, as if to confirm her surmise, and the startled ghost immediately fled.

If she wasn't mistaken, the people of this generation also seemed stunted. What could the reason be? Once these same people had unflinchingly sacrificed her for the sake of their own futures. Had her life's blood not brought them happiness? Had they failed to protect themselves from subsequent hazards?

The ghost's understanding of past, present and future was limited, so she had to rely on her feelings. She compared what she was seeing now with her own era, and tried to figure out what had changed.

The stumbling zig-zagging alleys and the ugly slump-shouldered houses, which looked like they had consumed whatever beauty they once had, were also found wanting, unable to cheer up the ancient wraith; instead, her spirit sank even farther. It seemed that the villagers of this age languished as they hadn't in hers, and it marked a general decline. If that was the case, what was the use of all their trappings?

She considered her short life and its pitiful conclusion. It was difficult to overlook the punishment she had suffered here. Yet, as the waves beat the coast, she remembered the beauty of the old village once more, and she was prepared in one breath to forget her black fate and the severity of her condemners, reconcile with the living, and even to support them. She wanted, however belatedly, to understand her crime, its consequences, and her sacrifice to future generations – no matter how difficult it was to do so. At present though, what she had seen here did little to comfort the eternally drowned woman. If further investigation yielded no consolation, better to have slept at the bottom of the sea and borne the weight of the waters.

But no, the bottom of the sea was not dear to her, and she would not voluntarily have selected it for her eternal rest – she was thrown there without any other choice. They had drowned her to cover their own weakness. Slaves of fear had sacrificed her to propitiate fear! She could not condone the actions of those who had condemned her to death as either wise or honourable – as they had simply panicked. Their fear had eclipsed wisdom, honour and even humanity.

They had thought themselves powerful, but their power was only sufficient to terrorize one weak woman, so they took vengeance on Aypi for their own cowardice. What a twisted world, where weakness spurred men to mete strife out to each other, with the mortal weapon of fear in their hands. Until they put it aside, injustice, tyranny and war would not be laid to rest in the world.

The thought of them infuriated Aypi. Recalling her own husband Dadeli, she tried to understand man's timidity. Had anxiety about their wives made them into dwarves? Like it or not, in every man's heart was the dread of being weaker than his wife and so losing her. This provoked them to their false bravery, brutality and inhumanity. How could women ever be content with such as these? How could Aypi, remembering her sad end, agree to silently dissolve into nothing? No, the regret from her life lingered in the living world, she could not leave it, that was impossible.

Aypi's spirit flew on its way until she was high above the darkened, run-down fishermen's village. It was small enough for a living person to cross and not run out of breath, and tonight it seemed as dark as Tartarus to Aypi – without any light, sound, or movement.

One doubted that it really was sleep. The fishermen's unnatural slumber looked as though it was but a hair's breadth from death's embrace. This was less of a village than a graveyard. Why were there no sounds coming from their dogs and cats? Did they too abandon their normal aptitudes here, or did they bark and meow on schedule now?

Just to contradict her conclusion, from below her, in a narrow alley, a wandering cat's eye gleamed, and a hound raised its head to woof complacently. It seemed that the village wasn't without cats and dogs after all, and the floating spirit realized that this age retained some similarities to hers. Of course, one wouldn't know it judging by the people – their anxious sleep disturbed and discouraged her from freely entering their homes. Perhaps it was better during the day, when sunlight would bring new colour to the inhabitants? What would they look like to her, who was so far removed from her own age, and what response could they find to Aypi's anger, the intensity of which alarmed even her?

7

At dawn the villagers went out to the salt flat situated on the outskirts of the town, rolled out their carpets and mats, threw down enormous cauldrons and prepared for the feast that would welcome the wedding procession once it arrived from the city. Even before the sun had risen high, there were signs that this party wouldn't lack guests, and already there was plenty of excitement and a sense of festivity in the atmosphere. Everyone involved outdid themselves trying to flawlessly perform their appointed duties. After all, was it easy to stand the scrutiny of such discerning guests? You just had to tighten up your belt, run back and forth from dawn to dusk for the sake of pleasing them, and be happy to be doing so. The villagers spent the early morning absorbed in these various joys and concerns. Soon though, they began to yearn for the arrival of the procession, and as the hours passed, they stared frequently and fixedly at the road coming from the city.

The wedding procession would come right down that very road; Mered Badaly's boy was getting married today! Actually, he was already married. It had been done last night at a restaurant in the city, but his father had stood up for himself and demanded that the kid display the bride to the village on their way to the bridal chamber. The bride and groom were compelled to agree. Their consent was not eagerly granted, as Mered Badaly realized from the prolonged and agitated whispering that first took place between the two young people, and then between the girl's parents. The villagers must have had some intimations of the precarious situation, since they nearly exhausted themselves staring at the road. Thus early morning passed, then came mid-morning, and then, lo and behold, it was almost noon. People began to furtively glance at each other for reassurance and out of speculation: Would they come, or not? Surely they had to come. If they didn't arrive when and where they were supposed to, had they purposefully delayed? What was one to think?

The sun grew hotter and the crowd cast ever more sympathetic gazes at Mered Badaly, and if one took a look at the host, it was impossible not to see the discomfort the party's delay was causing. As the sun neared its zenith, his face bore less and less of the morning's jubilation and ever more worry lines. It was easy to imagine that he was disappointed both for himself and his peers, since he was the one who had brought them and their children out here. If the wedding procession didn't come, who would be the scapegoat, if not the host? It was a terrible realisation for the rest too, who had anticipated so keenly what they knew would be the last wedding of this village.

If they had been in the village itself, perhaps Mered Badaly wouldn't have felt so guilty, but last night his son and the bride had exacted a condition from him: They refused to humiliate themselves by leading the procession into the village itself, among those pitiful hovels. Rather than bring their guests into the ridiculous houses perched on crane-leg stilts and listen to remarks of the newcomers asking incredulously, "Your parents live like *this*?" it would have been better not to marry at all.

At first, of course, Mered Badaly had been furious, after all who wouldn't be, hearing their dwelling place insulted in such a manner? As the young people became increasingly distressed, it was impossible for him, as a parent, not to understand that there was a secret behind it. They weren't being contrary for the sake of it, he had said to himself, as they furtively argued in the restaurant the night before. They didn't want to show every person who came along how pitiful the groom's parents were; if they did, it would just hurt their own chances. How could he not agree with them, and grant his servile assent? If you looked at the fundamentals of the matter, you'd have to say: "As long as the young people are happy, that's what counts. The rest of it – all the customs, traditions and practices passed down since ancient times, to hell's flames with all of it!" Mered Badaly though, feared it wasn't just a matter of setting customs aside, but a grave concern for the present and future. If the old man's son and his bride refused to cross the threshold of their own parents' home on their wedding day, how would it be later on, with their grandchildren? Wouldn't they repudiate their grandparents entirely?

Yes, the village was old; the houses were dilapidated wrecks without polished embellishments and brilliant furnishings of artisan timber like the city places had, but the fishermen's open hearts were here. Hadn't they made it for generations in these wooden huts? If they had a hardscrabble legacy from their ancestors that didn't figure in any luxurious lifestyle with unassailable wealth or beautiful mansions, was that the fishermen's sin? Why couldn't his son understand this, as if he hadn't left the village just a few years ago? Why did he take his new wife's side? If it went on like this, if he turned into her valet, what would be the end of it? Would he retain any mind of his own or end up completely under her thumb? No, he didn't wish to see his own boys so weak, but he could already see something different in their character. It wasn't easy for him to see that his words no longer had any effect on Kerem, but he consoled himself by imagining that things would change after he followed him to the city.

As he stood in the crowd staring at the road, the host's thoughts vacillated between anger and conciliation. His anger justified itself: So what if the girl was from the city, and so what if her friends were too? Why shouldn't they come to the groom's own village? Why shouldn't they cross the threshold of the hut he grew up in? What about good upbringing and respect towards one's elders? This was no way to treat the parents who'd raised him! Was it right for the child to toss his folks aside as soon as he stood up on his own two feet and began to take care of himself? Look at this, them acting as though their house was the poorest of the poor! True, perhaps they were poorer than the city people, but was anyone in this village poor by choice? Who didn't want to only drink oil, and only wear silks: to live the good life? Like all other people, the fishermen didn't see themselves as inferior – their potential, motivation and ability weren't less than anyone else's. They didn't want to fall behind the times and though their hard life hadn't made them weak, it had only given them a pittance; but what could they do? Cry and moan, drop everything they were doing and spend their life complaining? Perhaps, like pheasant chicks, they should disperse on all four winds and leave their village behind without a second thought? No, it wouldn't be like that – neither Mered Badaly nor any of the others could give up their beliefs so lightly.

There was no one here who would be able to leave the village easily, and when Araz charged them with that, he misjudged them. Mered Badaly had seen Araz observing them from the corner of his eye for a while, but wasn't sure how to open up to the man. He knew very well which of them had the right of it, but he didn't have the guts to join with Araz, stand up to the government, or go out to sea illegally: he'd grown old. If he were Araz's age, perhaps he also would've refused to bow. He was a whitebeard now though, and it wasn't for him to take to the streets; even if he weren't afraid and embarrassed, there were still things he could do, and things he couldn't do. From a distance, he looked at his wife Jemal making preparations, and his heart ached. Though he didn't recite her name with each step he took, he truly respected her. It was clear that she was unable to find a place between her husband and son, and it was making her anxious. The least the boy could do to comfort his mother would be to bring the wedding here.

He would not say anything on this particular day to offend the child he'd raised; in fact he'd take heed to moderate himself. If his son was not ashamed to shrug off the village of his birth just to please his bride, then that was his own affair, even if his father couldn't approve of this or support him.

It was spring now, and if the field hadn't been blooming with poppies, the groom's father wouldn't have tolerated having the wedding in this flat, barren place. One had to concede however, that the village's exterior was prettier than its interior. This place between the hills seemed like an ideal setting for hospitality and for celebrating the young couple's happiness. The weather was a bit hot, but not all the flowers had wilted, and there was still grass to be seen!

8

At that moment, a column of dust appeared on the horizon, as if it had just been waiting for the host to come to terms with everything. Among all the people assembled, there wasn't the slightest shadow of a doubt that it was the wedding procession. Even from a distance, the size of the dust cloud appeared large. What else could it be, besides the line of cars making their way to their village? Surely, the authorities wouldn't gather and come all this way on a day off. Mered Badaly didn't have time to collect his thoughts.

The young people around him cried out– "There they are! The cars are coming!" as they scrambled up the highest mound they could find.

Young and old sprang into action, as if they hadn't just sat baking in the sun for several hours already.

"We don't have enough mats, just look how big that cloud is! Can't you get another lot of carpets and some more water? Will these tea sets suffice?" fretted the organizers, driving themselves into a state of distress. "As soon as the couple arrives, put the food out in front of them, don't make them wait for another second!"

"Like we didn't have to wait..." grumbled Rejeb, who had volunteered to transport things back and forth in his car.

As soon as he said this, a cacophony of voices came at him: "It doesn't matter if we've had to wait; you can't make the bride and groom wait! Your own father put aside all care for himself the day you got married!"

"Well, we never do remember how that stuff happens," conceded Rejeb.

"Boy, if you don't remember, then it must have been no different, otherwise you would have!" exclaimed a wit from a crowd of women making preparations.

The entire group laughed at the woman's remark. The organizers, concerned with the size of the parade, wasted no time in getting some more crockery and water brought up from the village.

"Couldn't you bring up more chairs too? Doesn't matter whose door you knock on – these are city people, and they won't sit cross-legged on the ground, they need chairs and tables!"

Rejeb and his helpers promptly set off for the village. Man-Weli watched them as they departed. "How about that!" he said, slapping his knee, "How about that!"

"What do you mean 'how about that'? Say what you really mean!" laughed out Jemal, as she passed by.

"I'll tell you what I mean," said Man-Weli, adding his laughter to hers. "Will Mered Badaly ever stop waving that ladle around? His in law is almost here."

Hodja sneaked up behind Mered Badaly and playfully grabbed his hands.

"I've got you, Mered Badaly, go ahead and let everyone hear what you've got to say!"

Man-Weli cautiously backed away from the cauldron, and repeated the fishermen's old jest: "Can I ask, after five days in the city, has anyone there become settled, like us? No, all of them are still the same old shit-bottomed nomads as they were back in the day!"

Hodja roared and let go of the host's hands. Mered Badaly, while seasoning the food, met this joke with another:

"Don't speak in this way about my in laws, Man-Weli! Else they'll call you wooden-assed, and when you sit down you'll prove them right!"

Hodja broke in, "If they say that, we can't refute that: isn't it true that our bottoms have always been stuck to wood? We have spent our whole lives sitting in boats. Those nomads have the right to say that."

The clouds of sand began weaving in between the dunes, until finally the cars appeared in a long line before the crowd. An old man standing on a hill nervously muttered to himself: "Bless me, there's ten or twelve autos, they're not skimping on pomp. We might not have enough pilaf. I told ya like, I did, but Mered Badaly you said yourself there wouldn't be more than fifteen or twenty people, and told us not to worry. There are way more than that now!"

"Hey, keep your pants on until you reach the water! How do you know they haven't already eaten? Everything in due course! Don't we have some sturgeon set aside? Then we could also make some kebab or whatever and put on another cauldron of pilaf, if it looks like we won't have enough," said the old chef, placidly looking down the line of steaming pots. "First let'em come, then we'll see! It's our pride and duty to serve the guests at this wedding!"

A truck in front pulled away from the rest and came to a stop. Two young men jumped out to enquire of the old fellows: "Where can we set up the place for the guest of honour?" The moment they were shown the spot, they arranged the tables and carpets just as the line of cars arrived.

"Assalamaleykum elders!" called out the bride's father, Borjak Nurbadov, as he shook hands with the old men, starting with his new relative.

The other guests from the city accompanying him began to faithfully repeat his every action, ponderously shaking hands with all present. After the honoured guest was seated at the head of his fine table, the host situated several of his friends beside the new arrivals.

They all enquired of each other's health over the honking and hubbub of the procession. Meanwhile, the young folk who had poured from the vehicles, bored to tears by introductions already, broke out into dance as soon as their feet hit the ground. "Kusht! Kusht! Kusht depdi!" shouted one young man, using all of the air in his lungs.

"To celebrate this auspicious day, we have brought musicians with us," announced Borjak Nurbadov pretentiously. "This is no job for children! Your ears must be growing rusty here, aren't they?"

"That's for sure," said tall Hodja, pre-empting the host. "We haven't seen anything like this in years. Actually, they've just about cut us off from the outside world by now."

Nur Tagan thought that was a little too negative for a wedding day, and without waiting for Mered Badaly, tried to get the conversation back on track.

"Excellent thinking sir. They say the splendour of a wedding lies in music. We've also got three or four youngsters ready too, so let's combine 'em and they'll do wonderfully well together."

"'Prosperity always arrives with musicians and singers,'" said Mered Badaly, flattering his guest. "That is to say, you've come, and our prosperity has increased!"

The toastmaster came out with champagne brought from the city and deftly arranged some glasses amid the elegant table settings. After the couple had been seated, their glasses were filled, toasts were raised and accolades spoken. The wedding in the sandy expanse began to pick up pace as the crowd mingled and people took their places. The young people though didn't have the patience to stay sitting down for long, given the opportunity to dance.

After the bride and groom had joined the musicians robed in full costume, the dance circle widened even more until the noise carried across the whole field.

> *That sweet neck,*
> *Those two pomegranates!*
> *My love's hair,*
> *I'll kiss every strand!*
> *Kusht, kusht, kusht depdi!*
> *Hey! Hey! Hey! Hey! Kusht depdi!*

Produce from the city was added to the food that had been cooking since dawn both in cauldrons and in holes dug specially in the ground, amounting to a marvellous bounty. The villagers' mouths, which had recently become so used to deprivation, watered at the sight of it all: "A feast has come to famine's door." A good many fishermen decided that urban life couldn't be that bad after all. Maybe if they moved to the city soon, they'd enjoy many a thing their parents never had?

But watching the village youth mix with those from the city, the elders couldn't help but notice how readily they mingled. Mered Badaly spotted a particularly beautiful young lady because of the old-fashioned style of her dress and the remarkable ruby necklace she wore. He assumed she was a guest from the city, yet somehow she looked much more like one of their own. Her modest dancing confirmed this: when the city people danced, their movements were affectedly unabashed. The village youths were somewhere between the two extremes. Modest and beautiful though she was, the mysterious woman made Mered uncomfortable. He decided to observe her and having stood up from his place at the table he approached the wild dance circle.

As he got nearer to the crowd of dancing young people, they became as indistinguishable as the water in a wave, while those in the audience enthusiastically clapped their hands and shouted out encouragement. The whole village in fact seemed ready to burst from happiness and excitement, and even the worn-out old folks left behind at home like Kebe Ene had felt the energy of the gathering.

The younger villagers had already mixed together with the city guests, but the older folks were not to be outdone, and they too, one by one, came forward to dance, while those who didn't join in cheered from the side.

See – my love comes
On a silent horse!
If I grab that white wrist
I'll get a kiss!
Oh my soul, my soul!
That dark eye stole my soul!
Kusht, kusht, kusht depdi!

Apple and pomegranate blossom,
Fruits upon fruits,
Those eyes are a spell
Those eyebrows a dance
Kusht, kusht, kusht depdi!
Hey! Hey! Hey! Hey! Kusht depdi!

The festivities reached such a pitch that the toastmaster's throat became sore, and in addition, his speech began to slur.

If he had nothing else to say, he just exclaimed "all right then!" and stroked his locks.

With his hands behind his back, Mered Badaly weaved his way through the crowd, often catching an ephemeral glimpse of the stranger that only incited him to further pursuit. Each time he got near she seemed to vanish and appear elsewhere. She seemed more a mirage than a woman!

Unable to accomplish anything, he resignedly returned to his table. In the chaos of drunken revelry nobody saw him.

He sat down next to Borjak Nurbatov, but his accomplished in-law paid him not the slightest notice, but only watched the dancers, now and then glancing at his watch, or exchanging a quick word with the other city guests. He looked as if he were attending some unpleasant but obligatory official function and wished the time to pass quickly. Mered realized that nobody else at the wedding paid him any heed either; they were too preoccupied with themselves. In such a crowd the host felt like a fish swimming feebly against a current.

Mered tried to be as festive as the rest: when they raised their tumblers and champagne glasses, he raised a glass of water, took a bite of food, and hummed to himself or joked with Nur Tagan sitting beside him.

After a while he got up again. This time he walked away from the crowd towards the desert to relieve himself. Suddenly a teasing female voice sounded behind him. "What are you doing out here? Aren't you looking for me?"

Mered started in shock; he looked back and there was the woman, smiling at him. How was it possible? How conspicuous was her old-fashioned dress with its loose, archaic cut and antique fabric, and especially that necklace glowing like red embers!

"Who are you? What are you doing here? We built a ladies' restroom near the stage back there, there's no reason for you to come out here."

"I'm just a wedding guest like everyone else," she quipped, "you were looking for me, and I've decided to appear before you here. Did I do wrong?"

"I only came out here to attend to my necessities. I'll just go back now, if you'll give me a moment," he said.

"A moment, you say? I have a lot of time if nothing else, but never any necessities; not for ages anyway." Mered understood nothing of this. The woman questioned him again: "Why is the wedding taking place here in a barren field, rather than in our village?"

"Our village, is it?" he thought to himself. "How is it 'ours?' I've never seen this woman here in my life. Who is this and what does she have to do with anything?"

Before he could ask, his gaze fell onto the ruby necklace around her neck. His heart pounded and he was stopped in his tracks, just as if the beads had hypnotized him. How beautiful it was! Inside him a small voice cried, "Don't stand here with this stranger, run away as fast as you can!" His legs turned to jelly beneath him though; the jewel had enthralled him. "That wasn't my idea," he pleaded as a guilty child would to his mother. "If it'd been up to me, we would've had it in the village, but I had to compromise and settle for being nearby. Don't blame me," he said contritely, "I'm just here to relieve myself. Come now, it would be better if you went back."

He turned away and walked behind a bush. Soon he emerged and walked back towards the wedding, but astonishingly, the woman appeared before him again. "You had to compromise, did you?" she asked, staring at him.

"Of course! What else can you do? That's what you have to do in life, if you want to keep your family safe."

"When did you become so submissive?" Aypi asked, "is that what it means to be a man?"

"For ages now all we've done is submit. I don't suppose a young woman like you would understand that", he replied, not realizing to whom he was speaking.

"For ages?" she echoed, "Keep it up and there'll be nothing left of you! It'll destroy the fishermen and the sea as well – as it already has!"

"Look at this!" Mered complained indignantly, "I'm standing here learning manners from some girl, just like I'm a naughty child? You don't even know what you're doing."

"Whatever I feel like, that's what I'm doing!" Aypi responded warmly. "You don't understand what I'm capable of!"

His wounded pride spurred on the senseless argument: "Dear, if you don't want to be seen as a fool, stop being so high and mighty!"

"Oh really? You just wait and see what I'll do!" then she laughed strangely.

As she laughed, she vanished from sight again. He rubbed his eyes and glanced around to try and see if it was dream or reality, but nothing happened to clear up his doubts. Perhaps he was seeing mirages in the hot air. He returned to the wedding, sat down at the table in his old place and let out a sigh. He was barely able to absorb the party going on around him. Whoever it was, he'd never seen her in this village before, yet suddenly there she was! If a man lives long enough, he'll see every sort of thing!

He turned to his companion Nur Tagan and whispered in his ear: "Do you know where we are right now?"

Nur Tagan gave him a confused look, not knowing what to say. "If I'm not mistaken," he answered cautiously, "we're sitting out in the desert, but…"

"Yes, go on?" Mered said eagerly. "What else?"

"Well," continued Nur Tagan, "if you're checking on me, we're at the wedding of your youngest son."

"No!" he yelled in his companion's ear, "I mean, what kind of times we're in?"

"Oh, in that case it's the end of spring, and the beginning of summer! Can't you feel the sun drilling into our heads and boiling our brains?"

Mered shook his head. "Listen!" he declared, answering his own question, "we're at the exact midpoint between the past and the future! You and I are nearer to the past, so we don't even understand the present. It's like a veiled woman to us! Time has passed us by. Soon these eyes will see only visions from the past."

9

As the afternoon got on, Borjak Nurbadov begged for his host's forgiveness and, gathering up the honoured guests accompanying him, returned to the city. After that, the toastmaster became even more complacent and finally felt himself the true master of ceremonies.

Mered Badaly smiled at this – a game played by vodka. Could Turkmen hold any celebration without vodka these days? Among people like the fishermen in this village, you'd be hard pressed to find a single person who could keep himself from wine and spirits. As people would say, "If your neighbour's blind, start squinting!" and those present all observed this rule diligently: If the chiefs in the offices couldn't pass a day without it, what remained for the poor youngsters to do except to take an example from their superiors? After seeing the city guests off though, Mered Badaly thought it might be time to wind down the celebration. He went up to his son and whispered in his ear.

"Wouldn't it be a good idea to cut off the drinks? They're getting pretty stewed. Our Pirim's already wasted."

"Let it be and don't worry about it. They're our guests and they're living it up! These guys can outdrink a bull. There are boys here that drink just as much vodka as a bull drinks water, and by God you'd better believe it!"

"This sort of thing can't go on in front of the whole village," said Mered Badaly, shaking his head, "there are women and children around, see for yourself."

"God Dad, you're so depressing! What, do you think my friends will steal the girls here or something? It's not so easy to please them, the girl has to be like..." here he looked around for a suitable example, "like my bride Gul-Bibi!"

Gul-Bibi planted a flirtatious kiss on her bridegroom's cheek:"You sweet-talker!"

Mered Badaly, abashed by the display, stepped back. The young people from the city had seen the bride kiss her groom though, and began to chant "Kiss! Kiss! Kiss!"

After that tease, what else could the bride and groom do but embrace for a real kiss? Those villagers who had seen this city custom before, smiled. Those who hadn't, when they witnessed the bride and groom's lips meet so gracefully, opened their mouths in amazement. The bashful young girls in the crowd muttered "oh my!" and hid their blushing faces. Children ran over to see the fascinating spectacle, and the nearest, most enthusiastic observers cheered and clapped their hands.

A guest stood up at the head of one table and yelled 'Kusht Depdi!' again. A jubilant throng followed him to the periphery and began anew the whirling, circular dance with its booming music. The boys and girls from the city ran to their cars and took out fluffy, drooping *telpeks hats,* and scarlet *dons.* After they'd put them on, the whole scene looked like a film.

> *In our home there's sugar,*
> *Let it be honey, God willing*
> *For Kerem's first born,*
> *A boy, God willing*

The little rhyme amused Mered Badaly. Bally came up beside them and turned to Nur Tagan and the others."Fellows, look at these guys, they just don't stop!" he laughed.

Kusht, kusht, kusht depdi!
Hey, hey, hey, hey, kusht depdi!

The amplifiers, hooked by the long wires to an idling truck at the edge of crowd, did their work, and added even more intensity to the celebration.

"Yes, God willing!" agreed Bally halfhand. "Look at these clothes they're wearing, it fits them to a T!"

One of the village girls, Bagti, who'd practised a good deal, went up to take the microphone from the singer's hand, and adding her voice to the boy standing beside her, sang an old-style verse:

A camel comes to the stable,
That feather-plumed head!
Oh girl, I've fallen for you
My life's at your feet!

The singer who had come from the city snatched the microphone. Attracted by the beauty of the bashful village girl, he began to flirt with her:

"Oh, well done! What a good singer this girl is! Girls, come over here, all of you! Let's sing together; what's so special about the city girls?! There's no difference really!" He began to move together with Bagti in the Kusht Depdi, and as he passed by, put his lips against her ear: "You're good at other things besides dancing, aren't you?"

The girl recoiled as if she had been stung and moved away. Her cheeks, already flushed with exertion, grew even redder. Gutly alone saw this and rushed up to the singer and whispered something to him. The man responded by switching his own fuzzy wool hat with Gutly's. Everyone laughed – except Gutly, and a small scuffle ensued which nobody noticed except for the vigilant host. "What the hell," he muttered to himself, "is going on with those two?"

Soon Gutly had his hat back and the singer returned to singing with renewed enthusiasm. The presenter, brushing back his long hair with his hand, continued serving vodka and champagne to everyone he could. The singer's verses went on:

> *A fiery blush rises!*
> *She'll burn in love's fire,*
> *Dear Kerem's thigh-o's*
> *Will meet against hers!*
> *Kusht, kusht, kusht depdi!*

The old men looked down in shame when they heard this. The singer made an announcement on behalf of the toastmaster:

"Friends! There's no fish in this water we're handing out, but you can dive in and do the crawl stroke! Whoever wants to toast the health of the couple, come up to the head of the table! While our fine toastmaster is dancing from his dose of 'fishless water,' come get a taste for yourself!"

The toastmaster danced around the Kusht Depdi circle in reverse, carrying a fancy platter covered with full glasses, dishing out drinks to anyone interested.

"Humph," grumbled Mered Badaly. "These fellows don't know when to stop!"

Gutly appeared behind them.

"Let it be, Meret, if the bride's father doesn't mind then what's it to you, let 'em disgrace themselves!" he said with a slur.

"The bride's father is already back home by now", Mered Badaly responded coldly. "I am responsible for what happens here now."

"Now, don't worry," said Nur Tagan, who wanted to reassure Mered Badaly. "It would be inhospitable to be too strict. Everyone's got their limit. I can see that boy putting a lot of that 'fishless water' into his jaw, but let's remember the privileges of a guest. Nothing's gotten out of hand yet, so don't worry. It's true Pirim's completely smashed; it's a dark day for Toti-Naz."

The rejoicing kept going for hours. The youths from the city and the village were going all out, taking inspiration from each other, and dancing ever more wildly. If there had been another village within walking distance, the wedding would have woken them all up, but since this was the only one around, no strangers appeared. As time went on, those devoted to drinking looked as though just standing on their feet was an effort. The toastmaster, though, was unstoppable.

"Fishless water!" he yelled, wandering tirelessly among the guests.

"This 'fishless water' can go to hell, and us too" muttered Mered Badaly querulously, unable to restrain his uneasiness. "During the war it was enough to spin our heads, and run us straight into bullets, what'll it do to us in times of peace?" he asked, turning to Nur Tagan. "Before each offensive, it would be poured out, the 'dope ration,' they'd call it. If you drank the stuff, you wouldn't even know if you were alive or dead, or been shot through. How many boys died like that? There was a boy from Merv, just a kid really. 'Mered, you drink this. I'm ready to die, but I want to see where I'm going when I die. If I drink it, I won't see anything, and I'll just stumble after everyone else. I'd rather be killed by a bullet,' he'd say, 'than killed by vodka.' But each time, he'd be too timid in front of everyone, so he'd just hold his breath and swallow his dose like it was poison. Finally one day it did the trick for that poor wretch: While we were all taking cover, he rushed forward all by himself, heedless of the heavy fire, shouting 'urra!' He couldn't hold himself still or keep low, and no one could keep him back. After that I never saw him again, alive or dead."

Nur Tagan nodded his head. "For someone who isn't used to it, it's poison. It'll freeze their brain."

"When they handed it out, that was the point! Otherwise, who would run out into a hail of fire?" asked tall Hodja, who'd also fought. "These pups'll freeze their heads soon too, don't just talk, end the dance, let's not wait until they do it for you. Thank God that they haven't started shouting about the bride's virginity yet."

"Good grief," muttered Nur Tagan. The old man could tell that Hodja had angered his friend. God keep you from offending someone during a wedding. Though the dancers and their vulgar songs were in bad taste, as long as they didn't go any farther, they were above reproach, since every one of them was the bride or groom's close friend or relative. How could one risk hurting their feelings?

Hodja, reading old Nur Tagan's mind, tried to swallow his words.

"Damnit to hell Mered, if it makes them happy, then that's gotta be good enough for us. Soon the village girls will be into this stuff and maybe we can keep them from it, or maybe we can't. There's no denying it, we'll all be living among these folks. Then will you let all their stupid jigs and ditties offend you? Friends, is there anything left for us but to accept things the way they are?"

"I don't guess that there is," lamented Mered Badaly.

The boys who had been dancing Kusht Depdi began a new dance, which consisted of lying down and writhing grotesquely. The old-timers and children drew near to view the nimble revolutions of the dancer as he spun around, never quite on his back or off of it.

"What kind of dance is this? It's not Kusht Depdi," said Rejeb, coming over from the pilaf cauldrons.

"They call this 'break dancing,' uncle!" laughed one of the youngsters. "You wouldn't know it, it's cooler than Kusht Depdi; it's international. Kusht Depdi is only for Turkmen, so nobody knows it anywhere except Turkmenistan. In the city, break dancing's much more popular than Kusht Depdi."

"Do tell, young sir!" chortled Nur Tagan. "If it's for Turkmen, so it is! What do you mean 'no one does it'; why'd you toss aside what's your own like that? It's a long road; sooner or later there'll be a time for what's really yours. You too'll give up on this borrowed stuff in the end!"

The young fellow quickly backed away from the old-timers, then rushed over to join the crowd of dancers.

Tall Hodja pointed after him and laughed.

"Ha, what a piglet! Look at that! I say it makes no sense; in this sandy old place the Kusht Depdi step has always been good enough! Break-shmeak, it makes no sense, though it doesn't seem to go on so long as the Kusht Depdi."

> *Come to the marriage bed,*
> *The law of the wedding day,*
> *Oh, to feel the lover's arms,*
> *The girl's searing embrace!*
> *Hey hey, that's the way*
> *That's the Turkmen Kusht step!*
> *Kusht, kusht, kusht depdi!*

The toastmaster had been skipping around the dancing circle, grabbing vodka wherever he could find it, and distributing the next round of drinks. Now he took the microphone from the singer:

"Hey, go down a little farther, I'll bet her lap's searing too!"

Hearing this unseemly nonsense, Nur Tagan yelled into Mered Badaly's ear:

"Friend, it's time to send these ones on their way with some dignity left; if we wait much longer they won't go when we say 'go,' and they'll find worse amusements."

The toastmaster took the microphone from his hand and asked "Where's that pretty young singer? Come up to the microphone honey! We'll teach you the secrets of singing! Learn some modern songs! Don't waste your talent here! You've got your whole life ahead of you!" He turned to the singer from the city: "What was her name?"

The whole crowd at the wedding heard the answer of the young man:

"Bagti!"

The long-haired presenter shouted with a higher pitch:

"Come Bagti! Come, my Bagti!"

Gutly couldn't tolerate anymore. He left the table, despite the pleading of his parents, and tried to get to the microphone so he could protect Bagti's reputation. The other villagers blocked him.

"Sit down! They're our guests!"

What could be done? The wedding was over, and mischief was beginning. Nur Tagan glanced at Mered Badaly.

Blushing after witnessing the day's terrestrial events, the sun was beginning to lower itself into the sea. The host sighed, "Well they've come and we've welcomed them, now let's see if we can get rid of them! Worst of all would be to stand

and gape here while the women and children witness this spectacle."

Thus the village elders decided to see their guests off. Soon the city dwellers began loading themselves into cars in two's and three's.

"Who on earth," asked Nur Tagan to Meret, "is the man in sunglasses sitting over there?"

The host moved his old eyes across the rows of tables covered with empty dishes. "Which one do you mean?"

"That one there", Nur Tagan pointed at one of the few remaining guests. "Sitting alone in the midst of things. And you wouldn't believe it, but he didn't sing or eat anything the whole time; just gawked like a raven."

As if he had either a supernatural sense or a gadget in his ears that informed him that he was spoken of, the dark figure got up from his place and approached the two men.

Opening up his mouth for the first time, he declared "This has been a rather agreeable wedding! There were no undesirable notions and, above all, it was free from anti-social elements." He took a long, suspicious look at the distant village, and continued: "Let me personally congratulate you on hosting a wedding based on healthy ideas! Good-bye!"

The two old men were left perplexed and speechless.

"My god!" exclaimed Nur Tagn, returning to his senses, "I believe that these people can even control our breathing! I noticed that the dancers' clothes were fake, and it looks like some of the guests were fake too!"

One of the dancers passing by overheard Nur Tagan. "Of course it's not real clothing! The real Turkmen cloaks are expensive, and moths eat the woollen hats, so fake ones are good enough for us! Entertainment is more important to people than reality, old man!"

After the guests had left and the hosts were cleaning things up, Mered Badaly picked up a half full glass of vodka and poured it onto the cracked earth. "Enough of fishless water," he said to himself. "Hell, one thing's certain: Even if you don't usually drink it, have a taste now and it'd still push you forward for the charge."

"Even if you don't taste it, you'll still remember the past," laughed Rejeb sadly, rocking a little.

Mered Badaly shook his head.

"No son, I'll not drink it. 'When old men play, they call up storms.' No, I don't think so. Certainly these men've tasted the 'dope ration' quite a bit. Everyone has their own ways, and if we sip this poison, it'll come back to haunt us."

"It's not about the vodka," sighed Bally. "It's about orders. Without orders, we're nothing!"

10

In the "dark of noon" as the Turkmen put it, when the terrible heat saps everyone and draws them back home or into the shadows, a police car stopped next to Araz's home. Two men emerged from it and slowly, almost painfully, knocked on the door.

"This is Captain Nurjanov from the police. Is Araz Atayev here?"

"How may I help you?" answered Araz dryly.

"There are some things we have to discuss."

"What, exactly?"

"Life in general! What do you think it's about? You're awfully curious. Get dressed and come out, we'll wait for you in the car. You'll come to the city with us and talk to the colonel."

Finally admitting that the scene, rather than an unsettling dream, was an unsettling reality, he replied curtly: "Yes please do wait. I'll put on some nicer clothes, I couldn't go out like this."

"Your clothes make no difference at all to either yourself or us. Stop with all this chit-chat and come out!"

"What's this all about?" asked Ay-Bebek, peeping out from behind her husband.

"It's nothing new, just our old friends here to see me," he reassured her. "I'll have to go with them, but don't worry I'll be right back."

Soon the police car was speeding away towards the city.

"Dispatch, pass the word up – we're bringing in our 'customer,'" radioed the captain.

Two hours later they finally reached the outskirts of the city. As the car stopped at a traffic light, Araz, who'd become parched in the sweltering car, noticed an ice-cream stand and licked his lips like a child. "Comrade Nurjanov, with your permission could I buy an ice cream? Otherwise I'm about to dry up."

The captain scowled. "Citizen Atayev, are you saying you really can't live without ice-cream? It's no use trying to make light of this situation, you realize."

Later, the captain left him in a small room and vanished. The space contained only the essentials: a table, three chairs, a safe and a cabinet with folders visible through its glass doors. Two large windows with bars loomed over them. Araz went over and tugged at the bars, they didn't budge at all.

"Do you like it? It's perfectly sound, as you can see," quipped a plainclothes man stepping into the room. "This was built by Japanese POWs, crafty fellows who knew their work! In half a century nobody's managed to escape from this maze. If you aren't agreeable, you can vanish without a trace in here. I've no doubt you'd come to like the place too." Araz returned to the table and began to lower himself to sit down. "What do you mean by just plopping yourself down like a roosting chicken? Who told you to sit?" asked the plainclothes man abruptly, his eyes boring holes. Araz shot up again. "That's more like it."

The man carefully placed himself in a chair, then pressed a button on the table. Soon after, a prettily dressed young girl entered the room and put a tray down before him. "Comrade Colonel! Coffee and ice cream. Is there anything else?"

"No thank you," replied the Colonel in an authoritative tone, "that's enough for now." The girl left as suddenly as she had entered. The Colonel sipped on his coffee and poked at the little dish of slush with his teaspoon.

"Ice cream is troublesome here, it melts before you can finish eating it. Now, to eat your ice cream in Leningrad or Moscow! They don't have real ice cream like that here, and they never will," he said, glancing sidelong at Araz. "But what can you do? One's got to eat it anyway! I don't suppose you also like ice-cream?"

Araz gulped and swallowed. "Ah no, I don't care for it myself" he answered mildly.

"Fine, then I'll have to eat it myself, though really I'd prefer to just drink my coffee. In this scorching heat ice-cream is a real relief, but suit yourself." Just as if he were at a restaurant sampling the dessert course, he savoured the ice cream spoon-by-spoon, revelling in its cold refreshment, enthusiastically placing it on his tongue and closing his eyes as each morsel of the treat slipped down his throat.

Araz looked away at the blank walls. He noticed a stain just above and to the back of the Colonel's head, discoloured from the surface around it. "Whose portrait hung there?" he wondered to himself. "They must've had some reason to remove it. It's the only thing in the whole room that's out of place." After he emptied the bowl, the Colonel settled into his chair like a cat that had licked a saucer full of cream, sipping on some more coffee. Then, as if he were asking a child, Araz posed his question: "I won't insist on disliking ice-cream, but to tell the truth, right now I'd rather like to know who I'm talking to."

The Colonel's eyes first narrowed as if he were angry, then just as suddenly turned round as saucers. "Who asks questions here? You or me?" He took the napkin from the tray and cleaned his fingers. "You're overstepping your bounds, don't you think? Stand up!" Araz stood up. "Sit down!" Araz looked dourly at him.

"No more jumping up and down, I'll just stand."

The Colonel pressed the button twice, and immediately an ox-like brute of a young man came in and stood behind Araz. His fists were like sledgehammers.

"Help this one to sit down," muttered the Colonel, "but don't break the chair." With one hand, the youngster slammed Araz into the chair like a misbehaving child, with force that seemed near to crushing it beneath him.

"That's enough. Comrade Lieutenant, bring him an ice-cream, if you please."

"What kind?" the brute asked peevishly.

"Whatever he likes, that's what."

The athletic Lieutenant soon returned with a small dish of ice cream he placed in Araz's lap, then silently left again. "Eat away, brave champion," encouraged the Colonel. "Only, if you want to eat ice-cream whenever you want like me, do something honest and worthwhile with yourself!" Araz eyed the ice cream longingly, and then glanced at the Colonel. He decided it wasn't worth taking serious offence at these remarks.

"So I sit around doing nothing, do I? I work just like anyone else, take care of my children and… "

"No" interrupted the Colonel, "you don't! You're a parasite leeching off our Society. A freeloader! People like you are overturning our socialist society! If it weren't for the likes of you, we'd have already achieved true communism! Our socialist homeland has been giving you welfare for years, teaching your children, and what did you do while all this money was being spent?"

"I fish. I'm a fisherman," said Araz, despising caution.

The colonel rapped his fingers against the table:

"You're not a fisherman, you're a thief: a poacher! If you don't straighten out, you'll be peering out through those bars. A five-year sentence! All you breakers of Soviet laws are little fleas and bloodsuckers! So that you're able to understand better, let me tell you a story from years ago when I was working in Leningrad."

"Comrade Colonel!" Araz interrupted, putting the melting ice cream on the table. "You're a Turkmen, just like me, aren't you? And you have worked in a place like Leningrad?"

"You're the only Turkmen here," spat out the Colonel. "I'm a Chekist. We may be from the same country, but we're of different races, understand? You're an absolutely useless creature of a village. Whereas my homeland is the entire Soviet Union! Wherever the Party sends me, that's where I go!" He arose decisively and looked out through the bars on the window. He then continued almost tenderly, "Now eat up your ice-cream before it completely melts. You've got that Turkmen pride, one word and you're ready to burst with anger." Neither of them spoke a word and the room grew quiet for a moment. Then the Colonel returned to his seat and continued his monologue. "Now son, if you promise to clean up your act, you'll be able to go back to your family like nothing ever happened. Of course they're anxious about you. You're from the old fisherman stock, so I'll put it in words you can understand: Don't try to sail against the wind, but choose the right course and keep your sails trimmed; if not for your own sake, then for your wife and those little kids. The two of us aren't going to decide how anyone should make a living or where; it's all over our heads. In Moscow, at the Kremlin, places you've never seen, that's where they figure these things out. Our job is to obey and whether you like it or not that's our duty. We're Soviet citizens after all."

The Colonel did not anticipate the villager's response. "Sure, comrade Colonel, that's how things used to be, but now comrade Gorbachev said we can make our own choices about everything." The Colonel scrutinized Araz from head to toe, even his disreputable old shoes, as if seeing it all for the first time. He looked slightly askance.

"So what? Yes, Gorbachev is saying those things, who else?" growled the Colonel insinuatingly. "The long and the short of it is, we've found a little job for you by the coast. Just like before! We have no intention to take you away from the sea. You'll be a warehouse guard at the port. So don't waste a moment getting started, let me close your case; it'll be the best for us both."

Araz took a deep breath, "I won't leave my village," he said.

"Why not?" inquired the experienced Colonel with a somewhat allusive undertone; he was in no rush to get angry. "If life demands it, what can you do? You're already past thirty, a settled man, but you are still acting like a kid. Are you forgetting that you have children of your own? Don't you know how difficult your situation is? We know more about it than you do. For example, everyone else in the village is sick and tired of you; they won't even invite you to weddings anymore: You weren't invited to Mered Badaly's. You're a nobody now, comrade. Araz Atayev, if a man doesn't listen to good advice and behaves as stubbornly as you, there comes a day when he ends up all alone."

"No, it's a lie!" protested Araz. "I would've gone to the wedding, but something came up and I couldn't." He remembered what his wife had said, and now regretted this.

"So now you'll try to throw me out of my own village because I didn't go to one little wedding? I've got to give up everything I've ever known or had just for that? The place my parents grew up? The place where their graves lie? Betray all that to become a useless wanderer?"

The Colonel was running out of patience listening to all this. He rose to his feet, with his hands gripping the edge of the table, then paced the room thoughtfully with his arms crossed behind him. He went up to Araz and whispered in his ear: "Stop parroting that over and over again! It is a tendency of which I am well aware. Don't you ever get tired of it? If those graves are so important to you, fine, let's relocate those as well. There's no problem for us, either before or after you leave yourself. And we can move Aypi's grave too, if you want. They say everyone's so afraid of her there that no one can sleep."

"Aypi has a grave?" wondered Araz, "they say she was never properly buried."

"Nothing is beyond us!" replied the Colonel emphatically. "If necessary, tomorrow we can find her grave wherever you like. See if I don't, but stop your foolishness, so that you don't make trouble for the everyone."

"Why should we be the ones causing trouble?" asked Araz, stroking his chin. "You're the ones causing trouble for the village; we just want to stay put. If you let us mind our own business, that's fine by us."

"Listen here," said the Colonel loudly, to make sure it got through, "If you don't stop stirring up trouble and agitating people against the government, you'll be criminally charged under the articles of the legal code dealing with social parasitism and hooliganism. Actually that's what my Leningrad story is about. In the 60's, there was this

Brodsky fellow, a real parasite you see, he'd write a line of nonsense, and imagined himself an unrivalled poet. So they got rid of him, threw him out of the country. Do you think it was a picnic? Eventually he took a prize from the troublemakers, and then he had no place in his homeland. In short, put yourself in order, or you'll wake up in Siberia!" The Colonel came up to Araz again, and stared right into his eyes. "Comrade Atayev, do you want to go to Siberia? Shall your children come with you or stay with their people? If you'd stop your idiocy, and I don't believe you are such an idiot, then think, dammit! Tonight you'll sleep in a cell here. Set yourself straight by tomorrow at any rate, otherwise it's on you! Clear?"

They put Araz into a cell and he passed the night on a wooden bench. In the morning, hearing that Araz still hadn't yielded, the Colonel gnashed his teeth and ordered the fisherman out of the city. The duty officer took him in a car and left him at the edge of the city at the crossroad through the desert to his village. They ordered him to go on foot only; boarding any vehicle was forbidden.

He began walking steadfastly, but soon the terrible summer sun peeped over the horizon. Occasionally a car would pass by without stopping, as though he were invisible, or perhaps someone back there had ordered them not to. He was alone in this unjust struggle, being beaten, and he felt on this day more than any other how harsh was their treatment of him. If only the whole village had stood up against this tyranny together, then it wouldn't have to be borne by one man.

By the time the sun rose, he'd already emptied his bottle of water, but he could only keep going forward. Though thirst and fatigue pressed down like a weight on his mind, he never forgot this. His feet were unwilling to take another step or carry his body farther, but he dragged them on anyway. As he staggered along like a scarecrow under the cruel sun, a car suddenly pulled up beside him. The driver opened the door and urged him in and gave him some water. He pitied Araz's terrible appearance, and asked him question after question, which Araz's thirst-swollen tongue could not immediately answer. When asked where he was going, Araz pointed forward. After he came to himself, he began to answer some of the questions, and explained quite simply why he was walking on foot in the deadly summer sun: A colonel in plainclothes had forbid him from riding in vehicles. The car stopped immediately.

"Brother, get out of the car!" begged the driver, "Out, if you don't want to ruin my life! I know I'm a coward, but I just can't carry you. Have mercy on my children; I have no intention of going up against the government. If that's what you're doing, then you're a strong man who won't need my help. You don't have too much more to go, just keep going on as you have been, and you'll be home. The weather will start to cool down in a few hours."

Araz left the car without a word. What could he say? The car sped away in a storm of dust, but after only a brief interval, went into reverse and came back. The man stopped beside him and opened the window. "Please brother, bless your soul, just please don't tell anyone that I gave you water and picked you up! You'll destroy me; I have babies at home, please have mercy on them!"

"Yeah, don't worry," said Araz, and the car revved and quickly sped forward into the dust again, vanishing from sight.

The next morning at dawn, with his feet as senseless as wooden blocks, he approached his home. With dimming eyes he saw Ay-Bebek staring at him as she sat statue-like on the front steps. She took him in her arms and painfully walked him up the stairs. She knelt down beside him in the doorway and began to weep. It was difficult to tell whether out of sorrow or joy – perhaps both. He tried to smile, but he was too tired even for that.

"Don't cry, I'm alive after all," he said, before losing consciousness.

11

At the first premonition of dawn, Aypi's ghost floated down from above and into the winding, dishevelled streets. As the sun rose in the sky to the height of a spear, the village, as it always did, came to life. Like sturgeon in shallow water, people went back and forth leaving wakes behind them.

Mered Badaly, smoking his after-breakfast pipe, was walking along the street when Aypi flew up to him and rasped in his ear:

"Men are dishonourable cowards! They play a crooked game and repress their wives!"

Mered Badaly started and peered around, then cleaned his ear out with his thumb. She wanted to speak and be heard, so she cried mockingly into the old fellow's ear, "Woman: the head! Man: the feet!"

He stopped short and looked around again. "What in the world?" he said to himself. "If a man lives long enough, wretch that he is, he'll see every sort of thing. If a voice speaks in your ears, how can you answer?"

The voice came again in his ear: "Man fears woman!"

Mered Badaly looked up into the sky, in case that was the source of the voice.

"A woman's ruin is her husband!"

Mered Badaly wondered who the speaker could be that was joking with him like this. Was it someone hiding behind one of the houses?

He leapt over to peek behind a nearby hut, but it was completely quiet. He continued on his way, puzzled. There weren't many up early as him, so it was remarkable that someone would bother him at this hour. "But who knows," he said to himself. "'Every herd has its culls,' and a village has every sort of person. We may be small, but there's no shortage of examples in town. We even have our round-heeled women, just like the big city. It seemed like the voice came from the sky, didn't it?"

"Hey!" he shouted, to no avail. "Speak up! Isn't that Toti-Naz's voice? No," he reassured himself, "I haven't heard yet that whores can fly, not living ones anyway; the dead ones are another story." The old man's thoughts made him apprehensive. "Black bird, black bird, knock on wood! I take it back!" he chanted.

After seeing how useless that woman's husband was, Mered Badaly wasn't inclined to blame Toti-Naz too much, and considered the fault to be her spouse's. There was no way to wash a dirty woman's face, but if she was dirty, the husband must have been unworthy of her respect. God give patience to the wife of a feeble man! A weak man will send a headstrong woman to run after everyone, even if she wouldn't have strayed of her own accord. Pirim's wife though, had no interest in labour, whether hard or skilled – just street walking. The woman had caught the thirst for money and would go to the city any time she could, then return like a snake in a new skin. People knew she wasn't earning an honest living, but who would openly reproach her or her husband? Everyone's troubles are enough for themselves, and Toti-Naz' infamy was a matter for herself and her family. There were many people who disliked it, but they simply waited for the situation to resolve itself, as did Mered Badaly. He reminded himself, "there's no village without a burglar, and no forest without a wolf". Else, the village's honour would rest on his and his contemporaries' shoulders. Everything was according to the times, and after all, was his own boy different from the rest? He didn't have the faintest idea of preaching to anyone now; he was happy as long as they didn't preach against him.

Really, in this place from which everyone was about to scatter, who was there who could preach to another? Most probably Toti-Naz was aware of this and did as she liked. Even her close relatives avoided saying anything to her face, muttering only "I've got no load on that donkey, what does it matter to me if it stumbles?" You could still find one or two who would burn with indignation in private, but that was about it.

The pipe-smoking elder's thoughts continued in this digressive train following the morning's strange events. "That's the way of life— when trouble comes, the strong weaken, and the weak succumb! And some women are susceptible enough!" Abashed by his thoughts, he glanced around furtively. "We saw war and famine," he thought to himself, "but we've never seen immorality the like of this age's. Yes, we always had one or two waywards, but they would slink by with their tails between their legs, around everyone else. Now it's the opposite. If it keeps on like this, soon the good'll have to feel ashamed before the bad, if they don't already. Maybe Aypi was the spark for it all. In the old days they said the troubles all began after she told our secrets to those others."

Absorbed in his thoughts, he knocked on Nur Tagan's door. After getting his friend to come out of the house, they stood together in the shadow of a wall. He filled and relit his old German pipe, which was a prize from the War. Over the years, the oils in his hands had polished the pipe smooth. After a couple of bitter puffs, he spoke his troubled mind:

"Tell me old friend, are women a bit weak, or am I mistaken?"

"Weak, of course," answered Nur Tagan promptly. "Man is man, woman is woman. Why would they be the same? Go ahead and put some woman on a boat and send her out into the storm. Will she cope? She won't. Everyone has their own place in life."

"Well," said Mered Badaly doubtfully, "no one'd want to trade them for their place. But why can't women endure what a man can, and why, when trouble comes, are females the first to bend?"

This time Nur Tagan thought for a while. This was a question he was, as ever, unable to answer.

"Hmm," he murmured, looking away.

Mered Badaly made his case: "Listen, this is what I'm saying: Wherever life's best, women always head that direction. Am I wrong? Think about it… if another village has an easier life, the girls want to marry into that village, and they usually manage it in the end. Another city, another province – whatever the case, if it's better they're looking that way. Good God, if this country sputters out and ends up left behind, the girls'll start heading to foreign countries! Isn't that a disgrace?"

Nur Tagan shook his head, "I don't know, I don't know, old pal," he answered, uncertainly. "A woman's weakness isn't so different from a man's: Heaven forbid either of them be weak!"

"You know, in the war," began Mered Badaly, "in the cities and villages we liberated, be it Russia, Ukraine or wherever, we found unsettling things. Our girls and women there would consort with the invaders. They befriended them and even collaborated with them. Whatever you may say, in my opinion, women buckle quickly during tough times."

"No," said Nur Tagan, staring at his friend with his sky-blue eyes, "I can't agree there. While the war was on in Belarus, we heard something: The fascists accused one village of helping the partisans, and marched the entire population through the snow, it must've been 60 kilometres! Most of the wretches didn't have proper clothing head to foot, no shoes or hats – you know what war is like – and when they got there, they say the only survivors left were women – the men had all died on the way from cold and hunger. What do you say to that?"

"I know what you mean," began Mered Badaly, "I'm-"

Nur Tagan, contrary to habit, interrupted.

"You're saying that women are immoral. But immoral women are another story."

"I'm not talking about the immoral ones," said Mered Badaly, provoked. "I'm talking about women in general. They can't stand hardship; they'll immediately throw themselves into the arms of the rich. I'm saying it's a result of their fundamental capriciousness! Otherwise why couldn't they endure what a man does? Why should they run off to the softest berth? The fact of the matter is, a nation's bulwark isn't women at all, but men. I realized this during the war, though before I would have thought the other way round."

Aypi was furious. "If man is the bulwark of the nation," she yelled down to them "then woman is the bulwark of life!"

Nur Tagan started a little at the sound, then muttered cryptically: "Speak the truth and be punished... what else can I say to you? What they say on radio and TV, or my own opinion?"

"Your own! I can get the radio's opinion from the radio, and TV's from the TV," said Mered Badaly, pressing him impatiently, as though this timeless question was going to be solved by his childhood friend in a poor fishing village on the Caspian shore.

Nur Tagan's blue eyes carried the sadness of centuries, as he argued with himself in plaintiff, helpless tones.

"In my opinion, equality has been lost in our age. The scale has tipped in the other direction. The breath of men used to shake the world, and they ruled over women, but now – it's the opposite. In this day and age, women do as they please. Do you ever see old men decide anything, as they did in Aypi's time? Now the government's in charge of it all. Honour is in their hands, and they put it to their own use. God forbid there's a disreputable woman; no good ever came of one! Right or wrong, the government'll take women's side. Who knows what the end will be? But one thing's for certain: the government has shackled man's authority for their own self-serving political ends."

Mered Badaly took a deep breath. "You're saying that the government has made men subservient? As simple as that?"

"You said it, not me," responded Nur Tagan, his eyes laughing a little. "What I'm saying is: anyone who flees their own people because they think life there is bad, is the weakest of the weak."

Aypi couldn't stand any more of this, and came upon them both. "Listen! Women don't flee from a bad life; they flee from those unable to make a good one! They don't flee from poverty! They flee from those causing it!" she yelled.

Imagining some voice in their ears, the two old-timers made to stand up and leave. "What can you say," said Nur Tagan "about the ethics of someone who decides that their own village is poor, and decides to move to another? Wouldn't a solid person stand up for his home, and make sure it didn't decline? There are people who run away, but who'd call 'em moral?"

This gave Mered Badaly pause as he recalled his sons in the city. Aypi, however, was enraged, and decided to wreak havoc on them all. There was no rehabilitating them; they were the same as ever, with the same old rotten thoughts! There was nothing different in their outlooks; it was all as it was in her day.

"Pathetic!" she yelled like a whip, "What gall! Men are all fools, and the root of injustice!"

The hovering ghost's bitter voice scourged at Mered Badaly as he went home. The unseen influence made him cringe a little, but he continued unaware.

"I'll make you all stare it in the face!" she yelled from above them. "Every one, top to bottom! Self-satisfied, pathetic wretches! You dare to judge women? You, the source of wisdom?! The judges of right and wrong? You, who see an unattached woman and stalk after her without a thought of your household, wife or children? Predators! You won't settle everything, no! Remember, if men are the bulwark of nations, women are the bulwark of life!"

12

With the wedding over, everyone returned to their never-ending daily cares. A heart-wrenching calm settled heavily upon the village. Araz too returned to his typical occupation.

Today he had gone out to sea at the very nip of dawn, and in the mid-morning when the sun began to heat up, he'd come back. Now he sat on the porch waiting for Ay-Bebek, while eating breakfast and drinking tea.

"Back, huh?" said his wife, coming out of the inner room.

"Yep. Go and send Baljan out, the weather's warm already, fish won't last long in this temperature. Yes, send him out, and then…"

"…And then, what?" His wife smiled coquettishly.

"Then the two of us will do some chores!" and he grabbed her around the waist with hands that still smelled of fish.

"Is that all you think about?" she complained, wriggling like something in a net to escape from this living snare.

"I think about a lot of things – you're forgetting the sea. If you weren't here on land, I'd be staying out there for weeks on end."

His words pleased Ay-Bebek on this fine morning, so she lilted back at him: "Fine, if you couldn't make it here without me, everything else's forgiven. Who cares about the sea?" she asked, her eyes laughing. "Maybe I'll make you forget all about the sea, and the fish too!"

"Keep talking, and maybe you'll miss all the morning's fun!"

Ay-Bebek set the fresh sturgeon fillets into the basket, which she then put into the hands of her son as he returned from the backyard. The boy, as usual, went skipping off down the street calling, "Sturgeon! Whitefish! Sevruga! Fresh redfish!"

"Yes, have him go and tell everyone, up to every door, but not yelling! Can't he understand?"

"I suppose it's always the same with children… when he sees that you've come home, his happiness makes him forget."

"Baljan!" Ay-Bebek called after the boy, who was already racing down the street, "one more thing!"

"Tell him not to come back until he's sold all of them!" yelled Araz from inside. "Even if he's got to hand them out for free, just as long as he takes his time!"

As soon as she came back in the door, he caught her in his arms and took her to the inner chamber. Remembering that the baby was still sleeping, she put a finger to her husband's lips.

In the late morning, Araz got dressed and went outside. Ay-Bebek raised an eyebrow. "Are you going out to sea again? It's midday."

"Nope, I've got to check on the boat. Start making fish pilaf in the afternoon."

"What's the point?" she sniffled. "You're always obsessing about the sea."

"Didn't I say I'd be back? I did, so stop your whining!"

In the summer, the only concern for most creatures during this time of day is staying alive, but people, as usual, manage to find some pastime for themselves even in the hottest weather. It had been this way in the olden days, when idle fishermen would repair their canoes and mend nets. Those old concerns were long gone now and most people just gathered for a gossip. Right now, as usual, they had gathered for a chat in the secluded place in the shadow of an ancient fishing boat wreck, away from their wives and children.

"Good day, voluntary relocators!" Araz said unenthusiastically as he passed by.

They knew from his tone and words that his greeting was anything but voluntary; still, they dutifully returned pleasantries. Nur Tagan was particularly amiable.

"How're you doing? Folks at home well?"

"Hale and hearty," Araz replied vaguely. "And if they weren't," he thought to himself, "are you the doctor to cure them?"

Nur Tagan, happy just to break the ice, continued. "Come here and join us for a moment, or have you really gotta rush? At midday there's nothing better than a shadow to sit in!"

"You keep hold of that shadow," said Araz. "I've just come for a quiet dip. Might as well try to enjoy the sea while we're still here. Not certain how many more days we'll be able to." They knew quite well what he was really up to, but he kept his secrets even so.

"'It's always a holiday with company!' they say, so don't be a stranger, son!" added Mered Badaly, who'd noted Araz's furtive steps.

Araz stood aloof for a moment. Then with his right hand he shaded his eyes from the piercing rays of the sun, and stepped towards the crowd. Everyone gathered themselves up as he, the one who had avoided them for so long, prepared to engage. They shuffled to make a place for him, but Araz remained standing in the sun.

"What do you need from me?" he asked abruptly. "Stop the doublespeak, and speak your part!"

They'd known he was angry with them, but they hadn't expected a confrontation, so this tack made them uncomfortable. No one spoke for a moment. Araz waited patiently and then repeated his question.

"What do you want? Everyone's already chosen their path: you're giving up on all this, and I'm the one who's doing the difficult work. You know this can't end well. Everyone's living by their own convictions, but don't think that the person going the other way is the soft-head."

Mered Badaly and Nur Tagan, disturbed, glanced at each other, as if to say, "We should've let this one pass by."

Bally tried to pacify Araz. "No one around here considers you more soft-headed than themselves, boy. In fact, we can see that you're more on top of things than we are."

Araz laughed sceptically. "I'm not a little boy you can befuddle with false praise, so stuff it. Instead, uncle Bally, tell me plainly: Why are you pulling a 'brave and cowardly perish alike?'"

Mered Badaly was unable to restrain himself. "If there's no hope of victory, why go to war? If we fall in with you, you'd lead us straight into the dragon's mouth, wouldn't you?"

Araz didn't like to speak against an elder, but he continued. "So, we're dealing with dragons now, are we? If that's true, why've you been telling everyone fairy tales all this time? What were those pretty words about? Money?"

"Look here, step into the shadow and sit down. Stop this nonsense!" said Bally, coming between the two. "If you stand there too long your head'll fry and you won't be able to go trawling! There's no fish on dry land."

The vein on Araz's temple stood out. All the pent-up anger and all the saved-up offence finally burst out.

"Don't worry about me, look after yourselves! Is it a disgrace to defend your home and lose trying? I'm not the one who believes victory is impossible, that's you. What farcical talk is this!? Wasn't poor Aypi herself sacrificed for this land? Who were the ones who killed her? Wasn't it us? And now, if after a century or two we've gotten so chicken that we're going to give it up willingly, isn't it a shame that we've killed someone for it? We're the ones making a disgrace of ourselves now, and of our ancestors too! Did Aypi go any more astray than we are doing now? One little woman, she just responded foolishly to some strangers' trick questions – as if she gave away some great secret! Her eye was probably stuck on that jewel too. But what's our eye stuck on, and why are we giving our home away to strangers? And why shouldn't we fight?"

Mered Badaly went into the melee against this unbending man. "We don't live in a fairy tale, boy" he spat, "so don't talk about things you don't understand! Has some enemy come here that we could fight and struggle against? If that was the case, these men wouldn't stand by! We're not intimidated by force; most of us are moving voluntarily!"

"I'm not your boy!" Araz railed with even more anger than before. "Your boys ran away, they're already city-boys; go and teach manners to them instead. Why'd they trade this community's future for good times? Now you're all running off to the city to follow after your children and grandchildren, is that it? Don't you know? All your hopes are bound to a willow tree! You'll never get 'em back! How can boys and girls, your grandchildren, believe in people who don't believe in themselves? You think they're waiting for you with open arms, but don't fool yourselves. The whole lot of you are only brave if someone commands you to be; otherwise, you aren't! Yes, they told us resistance is forbidden, but is it also forbidden to think?"

"Don't stand here raging against these old men, go rage against the ones making us move!" called out Pirim, who was barely able to understand the subject.

"Ah, one of the true volunteers!" Araz responded scornfully. "Pirim, you go teach manners to your own wife! Take a bottle of vodka with you in case you end up locked out, so you won't be without a companion.

Some of the younger fellows chuckled at this, but most of the listeners fell silent, since this time Pirim was taking their side. He, as though sensing their support, came up chin to chin with Araz:

"Why're you tormenting folk? Who do you think you're talking to?"

Araz bared his teeth. "Pirim, go take a seat in the shadow, or you might regret it."

The man wouldn't take the advice given to him. "Are you going to make me?" he asked, and suddenly swung his arm at Araz. As soon as a sledgehammer-like fist hit him on the chin though, he fell back into his old place. Rocking, he tried to stand again, but Gutly soothed him:

"Hold on there, Pirim. Stay here and take good advice sitting down!"

Araz, now thoroughly disgusted by them all, didn't wish to stay any longer, but just then Mered Badaly sputtered, "If we don't go, they'll throw us all in prison, say we're anarchists, dig up all kinds of things on us, and we'll have accomplished nothing! You spent a night in prison and what for? Is there any way to turn them back once they start something?"

"If I did, then I did, and so what?" fumed Araz. "If necessary, they can drag me in again. It seems like no one in the village but me has got enough guts to defend their own home. This

isn't about the government, it's about all of you, yes, you here.
When you change, the government'll change too, it has to!"

Pirim, red as a beet, clenched his fists and, as he often did,
broke in from an unexpected angle.

"We've got to destroy the seat of oppression! Mankind
must be rescued from danger!"

"That's right," laughed Rejeb. "But first you've got rescue
yourself from the bottle."

"You look out for yourself there, Pirim!" added Gutly.
"Mankind hasn't called on us yet! If we just manage to take
care of ourselves, that'll be an accomplishment."

"These days, if you open your mouth at all, it's a mistake.
Nothing better than to shut up," grumbled Pirim.

"Buddy," explained Gutly, "I'm not telling you to shut
up. Quite the opposite: As you know, everyone shares the
same fate in this world, but if you're going to get mixed up in
big things, you need some education, wisdom, and courage.
Which of those have you got?"

Araz, who had seen enough, got ready to leave. "I'd like to
tell you a secret," he said. "If you learn it before you leave the
coast, there's no harm. Good or bad, people've got to know
their history. If they lose their roots, they'll end up unhappy
for sure. There's a lot we're ignorant about – even the history
of our own village. Now, I've got some old writings on this
topic, and I've given them to Gutly. Sometime he'll read them
to you."

Everyone looked inquisitively at Gutly until he explained.
"I carried them to Ashgabat and gave them to some experts.
They'll return 'em after they're trans-literated: They seem to be
in Arabic writing."

Araz took his leave with as little warmth as his greeting.
"Gotta go. Sorry if I've gone overboard."

"No, there's no harm," answered Mered Badaly sadly. He observed the proud fishermen through narrowed eyes and recited, "'The water pitcher sinks in the water.' It isn't our words that'll sink him."

It was near high noon now. Like scalded lizards unable to bear any more heat, the shadows climbed into the bushes and trees and rolled themselves up under their leaves. The birds made strange, morose cries, and the ancient sea's white caps ambled in the moderate breeze, humming their old tune.

13

Aypi's ghost began her revenge campaign against the village men in earnest, spurred on by regret. At night, she emerged dripping from the sea before flying to the men as they slept, then stifling their breaths. The first to be punished was Toti-Naz's husband. Aypi followed him, appearing as a cackling devil, blowing sand on him, carrying him on the wind, and tossing him onto a trash heap. What little esteem he had in the eyes of his wife was lost, and in the end he could barely be considered a man. For the time being, he put aside roaming, and instead sat looking out his window into the darkness. The only thing the petrified fellow drank was green tea, and his recovery from alcoholism kept his wife at home.

"Do you have to scare a man to fix him?" complained Aypi.

This dubious success didn't satisfy Aypi's thirst for revenge, since she had no enthusiasm for training those whom she'd despaired of completely. Instead she followed them around after sunset, kicking them in the guise of a horse, pecking them as a black raven, buffeting them as the wind and hounding them in form of a dog. She was happiest when it rained: then she would humiliate every man she saw; stalk and disorient them or carry sleepers to the middle of nowhere at night, only to wake them up and revel in their confusion. She harassed them so much that they began to ask their wives which way to go any time they left the house.

The ghost pestered Mered Badaly in particular: "Look at this one," Aypi said, shimmering in front of him, "supposedly he went to war and came back victorious! But who was it that started the war, if not those like him? See this war hero? He's forfeiting his own country and yet dares to speak ill of women! He lives on the beach, but eats stolen fish! He's only providing a hovel for his wife! His ancestors lived in these same thatched huts! If your own home is no good, what's the use of being a war hero? Was there ever a hero who couldn't make ends meet at home?

The old fellow's life became a series of depredations, and he was so unlucky that he had to watch every step he took. Day by day, his desire for relocating to the city increased. In order not to become a living joke, he tried to carry on as before, but inside he was in turmoil. Finally he sent word to his son and made ready to leave as soon as he could.

Aypi, who had brought them all into such a state, was impressed by only one man: Araz. She had once considered him her greatest rival, since there was no way she could improve him. She had gloated since day and by night he was at sea, so it wouldn't be difficult to kill him, nor had she been averse to disturbing him as he slept. After seeing the other village men though, her anger towards him cooled daily. A pity his doom was already sealed.

As the days passed, Aypi played more spiteful games with the village. The fact that the pain she inflicted was felt by the women as well gave her no pause, desperate as she was for revenge. The unjustly murdered woman had broken the fragile barrier between life and non-existence; now her only thought was how to vex the living.

The exasperated fishermen became uncertain of everything, and didn't know whom to blame. Naturally, they recalled unpleasant tales of Aypi. In the end, Pirim, leaving the house in his wife's hands since he was unable to continue living without liquor, went out to get drunk. He stumbled into the sea and drowned, all of which was blamed on Aypi. No doubt she had sung some lullaby to stupefy him as he went under. "Otherwise," they insisted to each other, "wouldn't he have woken up when he fell in, even if drunk?" All they could do was send for his unhappy widow and little children to claim the former fisherman's body.

As the men became more helpless, it placed more burdens on the womenfolk. The fragile balance that had persisted in the village wavered, making everything confused and uncomfortable.

The punitive measures taken against an unhappy Aypi in a bygone age became a misfortune for the entire village. Terrors in the day and night complemented each other, until it was a case of the straw that broke the camel's back. Without any idea of the cause, the fishermen had no solution but to keep on suffering.

Aypi was displeased with the women also, who, in her eyes, were slaves to their husbands. She tried, however, to protect them. "In the desert, the mountains, or at sea, a woman is a woman and she should hold her fate in her hand. Why shouldn't she dress herself up and have fun?" she argued across space and time with the hard men who had punished her vanity so harshly. "Why shouldn't she turn men's heads and live well? Weren't we made to be beautiful, and bend men to our wills? Otherwise, what purpose do men serve?" she asked, knowingly. "Was there ever a real man who couldn't doll his wife up?" If you can't do it yourself, make way for those who can! If you can't love, step aside for those who can! When will men stop thinking of women as property? They want women to remain dependent all of their lives, only then they'll sleep peacefully! Just because they earn a living, they think they're the centres of the earth. They're so proud of their strength and intelligence, yet spend their days in fear of losing their wives. Instead, if they just kneeled before our beauty, everything'd be fine! It might not solve every problem, but at least they could sleep well at night. Was there ever a real man who didn't prostrate himself before woman's beauty?"

In what respect was a woman stronger than a man? When Aypi had been alive she wasn't quite sure, and she still didn't know exactly, but, if she wasn't mistaken, a woman's real talent was beguiling men. Of course, woman wasn't made for man's pleasure alone, but… well, in her own day she hadn't been against it. Her lures had been more than equal to the task of hooking Dadeli, the best man in the village! Her beauty had driven him mad! Yet, when he'd been caught between duty and her beauty, he'd betrayed the latter. His happiness had been stripped from him; he should have protected his wife, but his misconceptions of duty had been his misfortune.

Men bent the world to their desires, and women's foolish, pretty heads fell straight into their snare. Men struck out with violence, whereas women with deceit – though neither shied away from deception in time of need.

Now Aypi understood that gullibility had precipitated her tragic end. A woman's credulity, mixed with male pride, was a sure recipe for misfortune; but these were challenging issues everywhere, not just here. Everyone was trying to have their own way: just like the struggle between land and sea, it was without beginning and end, and with no projected winner.

A woman's magic lies in her beauty. Why shouldn't those weak in body use what weapons they had? What else did the all-powerful God and nature intend for women to do in this competition?

14

These days Ay-Bebek tried to live like everyone else, and sometimes she actually did. When Araz went out to sea however, there was no rest for her. Until she saw him safely back in one piece, life was all anxiety.

Today Araz had gone out just before dawn. After the wedding, he had no hope that his peers would change their minds, organize, or resist the relocation order. Rumour had it that on the wedding day Mered Badaly had remarked to his in-law, "we'll be in the city soon." Hearing of this, Araz had reviled the villagers to his wife. "Not a one of them would defend their home," he had assured her, and revealed his own grim conclusion: A people who would not defend their village today, would not defend their country tomorrow, if it came to that.

Ay-Bebek was not fond of her husband's increasingly dour opinions or his ever-lengthier trips to the sea, but she herself had advised him to go fishing instead of attending the wedding. Now she could say little in front of him, but looked disappointed and aggrieved nonetheless.

Naturally, Ay-Bebek hadn't lightly agreed to his trip that day, but she'd gotten a headache imagining a scene in front of everyone and was reluctant to urge his attendance at the wedding. Damn it all, if she'd known that Mered Badaly's illustrious in-law and his colleagues wouldn't be staying long, then she would have happily sent him there, instead of permitting that trip to the sea. Fearing that he'd do some hot-headed thing at the party, she had even gone so far as to urge him into the water. Now, if she were to nag him and tell him not to go fishing, it would be no good. If he mocked "When there's a wedding on, I can go out to sea, but during normal times I can't, is that how it is?", what could she answer? Tell him that she hadn't wanted him around anyone important?

"If someone makes one little mistake, it gets linked into an endless chain of trouble," regretted Ay-Bebek. That gratuitous error, which she'd let slip in the blink of an eye, left her helplessly manacled, so she had silently assisted her husband today as he readied his tackle – what else could she do? She couldn't oppose him; he'd simply say "Cut it out, I've had it." Oh, if instead of bothering him she could have convinced him… but what had once seemed possible was today out of reach.

"Damn it all," she cursed, "why does everything have to be so complicated? Will we ever be able to live in peaceful poverty? Everything we do turns out wrong. Things go from bad to worse, and misfortune seems to stalk us night and day with loaded weapons. How has it come to this? Where are the walls to protect us, and the sense of security that will unfold over us? Will it arrive just in time, when we're starving, or dying of thirst? When we're ill?"

"Is there any country on the face of the earth with secure, happy people? If you listen to the radio, things in other countries are very different, but everyone seems miserable there too. Everyone, from the cradle in their homeland all the way to the grave has to struggle and strive in this damned life. If you spin the radio dials or open up the papers though, everything's just fine: crops are planted and watered, bountiful harvests are harvested, and roads are laid. Life is just like a purebred horse galloping along, making you wonder if anyone can catch up with it.

Look around though, and there's a crude hut, or another shortage, and over there – a bunch of cowering people. How could Araz not be furious and bitter? Everything's just like it shouldn't be. Just as you grab it by the collar, the collar comes away in your hands.

Now we're going to the city and we have a slim hope that we'll live like humans, and that hope, however small, gives us strength. After we've arrived, there's no clear picture of how things will be, just speculation. When you look at city people, our little hope flickers out. Whoever has a big job lives well, but simple folk don't get along much better than us here.

Everyone's living in dire times, and there's no guarantee that things will be better in the city – after all, nothing is more difficult than the lot of a migrant: how much time is needed until you can adjust to new rules, find work and stand up on your own two feet?

On top of that, to be separated from the sea and taken away from the place your parents were born! To pass life far from this unblemished coast! There's a sea there too and they say it's the same as ours, but so what? Is it just about being next to salt water? No, it's how and where you live, that matters. Even if our houses aren't fine and it's not an easy life, this is still our own place, our own homes, and the place we were born. But there, everything'll be different and if we yearn for the sea, what can we do?"

She felt she understood her husband's distress. Perhaps Araz was the only one who truly anticipated the trials of the future, so he was listless night and day without the support of like minds. Nor was it a matter of fish, when he had said "I'm a fisherman, my fathers were fisherman, and I'll be one until

I die." His lands were being taken from him, as she well knew. If only she could have helped! There was no one among the rest of them who would stand beside him; they'd surrendered to their fate, so by comparison Araz appeared unwavering, relentless, and even contemptuous. What else could explain Araz? He'd grown up with the fire, but inherited the ashes. The villagers disappointed him, so he distanced himself from them. Dear Lord, what would be the end of it?

15

As Aypi stalked through the village, it became more and more deserted. This was a surprise, but it didn't placate her. She flew back and forth looking for victims like a poacher. Her purpose was to make men stare their own weakness in the face and temper them with the understanding. Instead of being tempered, however, they hid at home, it seemed, and their wives did nothing to chase them away. This infuriated Aypi even more.

Some evenings Aypi would see youngsters going to meet their sweethearts. These she never laid a hand on or terrified, rather she felt close kinship with them. Though she had married in her time and lived as the wife of Dadeli, she had never known love's pleasure in her life and still regretted it. Lovers to her were as sacred as holy pilgrims.

One night as she stared into the dark, however, and saw Gutly rushing somewhere, she altered her resolution and decided to follow him.

Who knows why she looked twice at this dandy of a young man? Perhaps the youth's beauty challenged even her despair and cynicism. In any case, though she wanted to teach him a lesson, there was something more to it.

She followed him to the outskirts of town, unable to imagine who he was hoping to see out here, but expecting that no prey could long resist the skilled hunter's charms.

Gutly finally stopped at a stunted little mulberry tree at the edge of town. The door of a nearby house soon opened and a girl's tall form emerged. She hesitated a moment, glancing around warily like a gazelle at the water hole before walking to the tree in the moon's pale light. Aypi immediately knew her, it was the singer Bagti, Aman-Weli's young, beautiful daughter, whom Aypi had seen perform at the wedding.

As she arrived under the tree Gutly embraced her. The encounter was brief but passionate, and even the lifeless ghost blushed and was unable to look away. Finally, the lovers parted hands.

"I've got to leave, Mom will be looking for me" said Bagti in a husky whisper.

Gutly began to return home. Without having any particular goal, Aypi followed the love-struck and oblivious youth once again, watching as he wandered along the coast in the moonlight, while she reminisced about her own era's vanished sensibilities. At last, she decided what sort of game she would play. She appeared before Gutly just as he turned to leave the abandoned coast.

The astounded young man stepped for a moment before he recognized the person before him.

"Bagti dear!" he said, "How did you get here? I thought you'd stayed at your house!"

"How do you suppose I got here? I ran!" said Aypi, mimicking Bagti's sweet tones. "I wanted to see you so badly my heart ached, I nearly died!"

"And you didn't think I wanted to see you too? But you're only seventeen, you shouldn't leave the house at night. If your mother or father woke up and realized you were gone, you know what a fuss it would cause?"

"Oh they won't wake up," said Aypi, forgetting for a moment who she was pretending to be, "they're all long dead and gone I'm afraid."

"What?" Gutly demanded. "What happened? They were fine just a while ago, what could've happened to them since then?"

"Sorry, I meant they're sleeping like corpses," said Aypi, remembering herself.

"Okay then," said Gutly with relief. "I nearly had a heart attack, I couldn't imagine what happened after I'd just been over there."

"These men, always thinking about themselves all the time!" said Aypi to herself. "Didn't consider what everyone would start saying about the girl."

Then she decided to test the strength of Gutly's love. She came up to him, ran her hands around his back then clasped hands with him, playfully entering his embrace until her lips touched his ears. "Dear, when will our wedding be?" she whispered breathlessly.

Gutly tensed up suddenly like he'd been struck. "Well," he said, clearing his throat, "I just said this coming year honey, while we were under the tree, have you already forgotten? At New Year's I have a break from university and you'll be of age, so if your parents give permission then we'll be married.

"And if they don't? Then what?"

Gutly couldn't answer this question, but he took his hat in his hand and looked away for a moment. The light of the moon showed the panic in his eyes. "Oh, it won't make any difference. We could get married tomorrow too."

"You swear? Really? Tomorrow?" she asked in her melodious voice, looking up and clapping her hands together.

"Yes, tomorrow," said the youth, smiling awkwardly. "As long as you're of age. You're the most beautiful girl in the world to me."

"Even in the capital?" teased "Bagti."

"Yes, even there."

"I don't believe you!" she contradicted. "There must be at least one in the capital!"

"Yes, yes!" said the slightly flustered Gutly. "I mean… no! You're the only one I love! That's all there is to it."

"Come on, let's go walk along the shimmering moonlight together," she suddenly suggested as she stood in the silver light. "Look, there's no-one else living nearby, if it's just the two of us, it's ok! Let's go! I said let's go! Why are you standing there like a post? Come on, let me pull you over those glowing waters!"

"Over them?" asked Gutly looking surprised.

"Oh what a bore! The moonlight! Its mystery gives me power!"

An inexplicable fear rose inside Gutly. All that his ears heard and his eyes saw were like a dream. Was he really awake? "It's like I don't even know you Bagti," he said fearfully. "You're usually so shy, at Kerem's wedding your singing was so bashful and so sweet. What's happened to you tonight? Are you feverish?" he asked, cautiously pressing her to himself. "Let me kiss you."

The false Bagti scoffed and laughed, "Don't worry, now it's my turn to kiss you!"

This truly astounded him, never before in his experience had a girl been so forward or said "I'll kiss you!" The girl didn't wait for his response, but violently pressed her lips against his, which they met like cold embers. When she finally stopped and stepped back, Gutly was unable to hide his delight.

"Bagti dear, I feel like a feather in the wind! You make me so happy!"

"Love gives you wings!" said Aypi, laughing at him, "so become light as a feather! Look, now open up your eyes, but fall sleep!"

Aypi lifted her feet off the ground and floated above the shoulders of the sturdy youth who floated right behind her. "Wow, those stars are as big as apples," he said as they broke through the clouds. I want to go see them!" he exclaimed innocently like a child.

"Be patient," replied Aypi, "they'll all be yours soon." Before they reached the heavens though, they alighted on Aypi's Island. Gutly moved to embrace her again but false Bagti slipped out of his embrace like a snake to stand beside him. Gutly took off his hat, and kneeled before her like a feudal lord.

"In this world or the next," he said, "I am yours! Tonight your white face is whiter than before, whiter than snow! There is no one alive with as beautiful complexion as you!"

"You've got that right," answered Aypi sorrowfully. "But I've got something to show you on this island that will frighten all these sweet words right out of you. Hang on to your hat and keep your eyes open! You're about to see the Venus Star, my love!

They flew up again, right into the heavens this time, and soon landed in an Edenic garden redolent with the birdsong of fairytales. To behold the creatures of this garden was simply astounding! Brilliantly coloured butterflies and scarabs buzzed around them, all astonishingly beautiful. Beasts, both predator and prey lived together in peace – the fearful lions and tigers with the gazelles, onagers, saigas, camels, oxen and cows, leaving them completely untroubled. All kinds of animal, bird, or plant could be found in the garden, and its grasses and the behaviour of the beasts amazed Gutly.

Monkeys leapt from tree to tree, gathering ripe fruits to give to the tigers, lions and crocodiles, which ate them up without any need for meat at all. The mountain goats had their fill of green grass and whenever they began to head-butt each other out of selfishness, the lions and tigers interceded to calm them down.

"What a beautiful place!" exclaimed Gutly.

"This is Venus!" she answered. "Life is such in this particular world."

"But why is it not like this in ours?"

Aypi reflected, unable to answer for a while. "I don't know; some mistake must have been made at the birth of our world perhaps? Maybe man can fix it before it's too late. That is, if they want to keep on living.

"Since we have come all this way, I'd like to see God, if that's possible. He's got to be here on Venus, right? I want to ask God himself one difficult question about mankind: "What went wrong on Earth? When will war come to an end?"

"How presumptuous you are! Do you think God is like a beautiful girl who will sit there listening to whatever you say and be happy with it? God isn't here, he's on Sirius. No one living can see him, only the dead! What's the use of only seeing the dead, if he won't speak to the living? Perhaps men are their own little gods! The best thing they can do for their lives is constantly improve themselves. Is there some other solution? No, only man can make man happy."

"How?" asked Gutly, as if suddenly waking from sleep.

"At the very least, if they don't do evil to each other, that would be enough to make them happy" Aypi replied with annoyance.

"Oh my Bagti, we're happy aren't we? We'll be happy and grow old together and then die someday, won't we?"

Aypi's countenance changed as she heard this. "A fairy tale," she answered. "Meant for children and young girls, not me. I'm not your happiness, and I'm not your Bagti either!"

The ghost's voice sounded sharply in his ears. "I'm not like the girls who've fallen under your spell! I'm the bitch inside every woman – Aypi! Have you heard of me?"

Gutly's eyes widened, but he was still obviously asleep, and he moved like he was swimming through a lake of milk. Aypi, realizing her hatred was useless, relented a bit.

"See the bird singing on the branch over there?"

"Yes, I see it," replied Gutly, who found the singing pleasant. "The song of those birds is like the voice of the most beautiful girls in Ashgabat!" He realized the slip, and continued "Just like your voice!"

Aypi smirked just like a living woman would: "If you went to Ashgabat right now, would you roam the streets, or go right to your dear Bagti? Come, it's time to choose your path!"

"I'll have to decide when the time comes… and so what? Always decisions! I still have to finish school, then I'll figure it out, until then I'm free to have a little fun like everyone else, I've got the right don't I?"

"Do you really? Free just like everyone else? You'll pay for this! Even if I don't help the rest of the village, at least I'll help one girl, or maybe I won't even do that, but I'll open the eyes of men everywhere, they'll finally understand what they are at least!"

They soon began their dangerous flight home through the cold darkness of the heavens. The terrified, sleepwalking Gutly finally landed on the Caspian coast. "Get out of my sight! Don't let me see you here again!" she warned him.

As Gutly woke up, he repeated the words twice. The first time he was walking like someone just woken from his sleep, but by the second time he was already running at full speed. In the feeble light of dawn his hat bobbed in the dark, flying like the birds in the dream. Aypi sighed, "Perhaps it will be a lesson to him," she thought, "Helping just one girl would quench my anger."

Gutly couldn't even leave the house for a few days after the incident. When she saw this, Aypi said "What a strange boy! And to think his fine words could befuddle a girl so."

"Damn them," she complained. "Have they lost all self-respect, that they can't even step outside? Is it possible? Where is this prodigal strength and spirit of theirs? What does it mean, when one little woman can take out a whole town of strong men, who've braved storms and raging seas, and turn them into house pets?" Should she rejoice or mourn? Did this ghost, both killed and brought to life at critical moments in the village's history, have any reason to rejoice in her work? If her deeds harmed these people again, what a pity it would be.

How to snap them out of it, she puzzled to herself, and return men to their natural condition? What was the source of their discontent? Why did they make their wives bow and expect some confirmation of their manhood? Why did they still brag of their lifelong dominance over women, when they too were born of woman? When little boys get into trouble, they hide under their mother's wings remaining dependent as long as they stay there. Perhaps pride made them pose before women to cover the embarrassment of that initial weakness and show that they counted for something. It was nothing more than men struggling to prove their independence from their mothers. Could this congenital guilt be the wellspring of their overweening pride and belligerence? How could they be cured of this stunting and made free?

If men recognized this unshakeable truth, they would recover from the ignominy and mend their courage. As long as they thirsted for war they were boys; to become men only when they disavowed it. The tension of birth, when they had hung perilously between life and death, still loomed in their sub-consciousness, and until that was alleviated too, they wouldn't be real men.

When Mohammad declared in the Hadiths that "Paradise lies under the feet of mothers," had he not only honoured the eternal role of women, but also shown males how they could be real men and true adults? Her grandmother Anna, a Cossack enslaved in Saklab and sold through Persia to the Caspian coast, had insisted that the Christian prophet Jesus said the same thing.

Regretting her own cruelty, Aypi lowered her head. As she ceased her flight through the village, she looked back towards the sea.

She had wandered the heavens for a time, but the peace she could not find on earth would not be found in heaven, so she descended once more into the sea, where her bones had rested in the sediment for hundreds of years, and took her uneasy rest.

16

With her heart in her mouth, Ay-Bebek stepped outside. As if for the first time, she took in the winding rows of familiar, run-down houses and huts standing incongruously but jauntily on frail stilts. Then she went back home and opened up her old hope chest, took two pieces of paper from it and folded them into her handbag. She took the baby up in her arms and carried him outside.

"Baljan! Baljan!"

"What is it, Mom?" he asked, as he came running from the backyard where he had been playing.

"Come and follow me!"

Together they left the village. She observed the wilting flowers and mourned the receding tokens of spring, which so recently had been poppies sparkling like red gold; just as she mourned her distant girlish dreams, long since turned to ash.

"Where are we going, Mommy?" asked Baljan tugging at her hand after they had walked for a while.

Ay-Bebek pressed on a little farther, then pleasantly answered, "My dear child, we're going to see our new house in the city. Look, here's the deed for the house," she said, indicating the paper's edge in her bag. "I've had it in my chest the whole time. Everyone else has seen their new house, so now it won't do for us not to see it. I've brought salt folded up in this hanky, and we'll leave it at our new house."

"Why?"

"How should I know? It's an old superstition, son. Whenever people move to a new house, first they leave salt in it."

"Mom, but why?" he echoed in his high-pitched voice.

"If you do, your new house will be happy and prosperous. They say it'll be a lucky house."

Baljan thought for a while, then, looking his mother up and down as she walked beside him, asked the guileless question of a child:

"Mom, will Daddy come later? Does he know we're going to the city?"

Ay-Bebek tried to assuage his doubts. "He'll know for sure, boy, is there anything he doesn't? He'll come back from fishing and see that we're not home, and he'll know right away we went to put salt in our new house."

"Mommy, let me go back and get him," he suggested, looking back anxiously at the distant village and obviously dissatisfied with his mother's answers. "Otherwise he won't find us and won't know where we went. Mom, if he doesn't find us, he'll be upset."

"He won't be upset! Why should he be, are we doing something to be upset about?" answered his mother curtly.

"Mommy," said the boy, staring up at the sky, "Look!"

Ay-Bebek looked up. "Why, what's up there?"

"Don't you see, Mom– over there – don't you see that black cloud? If the weather turns bad, daddy will come back tired. What'll happen if you aren't there, Mommy? Let's go tomorrow to the new house, all together."

Ay-Bebek's step faltered.

"That's hardly a cloud, more like some feathers that fell off a coot and are floating around."

Nonetheless, after that she ceased making any further progress: First she'd start toward the city, then back towards the village. Finally, shifting the baby in her arms, she resolved to turn around and retrace her steps.

"Okay then, don't fall behind me! Let's walk fast, if people are putting tarpaulins over their houses we'll do it too, otherwise, before your daddy comes rain'll be in our house again, and soak all our things."

"Okay Mom!" said the boy, happy to be going back. He went ahead of his mother, skipping just as he always did.

When they returned home, the black cloud growing over the sea didn't appear too threatening. Ay-Bebek let the boy go off and play and she put the baby in its cradle, then leaned over to nurse for a while. Her eyes, tired of looking for her husband's form on the road, involuntarily closed and she drifted into unsettling sleep.

Her sleep was not long; rays of sun reflecting off polished armour and weapons soon awoke her. From the sea, they crossed over the dunes, line by line: strange, terrifying warriors. They appeared suddenly, as though sprung from the earth, the limit of their massed formations beyond the range of sight. Ay-Bebek observed them from afar, wondering where they had come from. Just yesterday and even today, whatever else had been happening, it had been peaceful; everyone had been gathering up their children and preparing to relocate. Now the rocky, secret bathing places where so recently she had stripped and entered the sea were full of endless companies pouring out and dispersing from strange ships.

Ay-Bebek began sprinting to tell the village men, but her knees knocked; no matter how hard she tried, she could not run. At every step she tripped and collapsed. She couldn't understand how so many potholes and bushes had appeared on the well-known road, but each time she fell, she got up and kept going. How she suffered; falling, rising, until at last, when she hadn't the strength to stand, she crawled. "I'll have to go on this way," she commanded herself. The village was a distant speck though; how could she crawl such a long way? No, that would not stop her, but how painful and difficult it was, and her knees were raw. Anyway, that was nothing, because those stone-faced warriors, steel clad and armed to the teeth, were marching over the dunes, getting closer with each breath.

"As long as I get the news to someone, what does it matter if I die? Isn't there be some child or youth on the road who could go faster?" she wondered, hastening her crawl. At the crest of each dune, imagining herself near the village, she craned her neck and looked forward, then twisted around to see how much distance remained between her and the pursuing hordes. With each passing moment, the distance closed. She had little doubt they were foes: hunting her down this way, who else could they be? They were here to take the fishermen's village, and they wouldn't make any distinction between old and young, no, they'd kill everyone. Where was Baljan? Oh, and her poor baby was sleeping on the porch! If their eyes should chance on the crib!

Just then someone standing over her laughed scornfully.

"Why do you flee? They won't harm us! Don't you see me unafraid here? If it were frightening, I too would flee. If you don't curse them, they'll offer you a gift."

"Who are you?" asked Ay-Bebek, looking up at the woman. Getting up to her feet, she again enquired, "Who are you? How do you know these people?"

The unfamiliar woman's beautiful hazel eyes sparkled merrily. "Don't you know me? Your husband is a friend to mine. Do not fear them! Look at this ruby necklace! Would you like to try it on?"

"No!" yelled Ay-Bebek shrilly, "I won't wear it, I don't want that kind of thing!"

"Won't you?" mocked the woman, laughing. "If I give it, well, then you'll wear it!"

Ay-Bebek's eyes bulged looking at the woman. "Are you Aypi?" she gasped.

A strange sparkle appeared in the apparition's eyes. "Yes, I'm Aypi. Why didn't you recognize me? Don't play dumb, I know you did, if your husband does, so should you! All you people do is talk of me day and night. As if you yourselves were any different from me. How are you better? When will you see how crooked you are? Sooner or later you'll leave the village and be lost forever. You'll blame me for that too, I suppose? Did I tell you to do that?"

"Dear cousin!" begged Ay-Bebek, "I'll say nothing against you, but please help me escape these invaders! Let's tell everyone they're coming, if we go together, they won't catch us!"

Aypi glared first at Ay-Bebek, then at the multitude drawing nearer with their metallic clamour. She looked down, then snapped her head straight up with an air of decision.

"If you can't doll up a woman, it's no use being jealous of those who can!"

"Who's going to doll me up? I'm not a doll; I'm a living person. Are you speaking to me?" asked Ay-Bebek, dumbfounded.

"No, not you, but to these wretches. They blame their own cowardice on everyone else, but never themselves!"

Ay-Bebek begged again, "Dear kinswoman! If you'll pardon me, this isn't the time to take offence. Come, let's get out of here! We've got to warn the village!"

Aypi looked at her with contempt, and shook her head.

"Whether we warn them or not, what can they do about it? They won't even have time to get scared. I say let them all die.

They aren't even alive; they just sit there and gossip anyway. I'm tired of them. Aren't they the ones who made ashes of my precious life? The scoundrels," she laughed uncannily, "they blamed me for their own sins, they yoked me with all their guilt, as though they were lambs themselves! But I wasn't the one that brought these troops in the first place or now! If you go and tell everyone they're coming, they'll blame it all on you. That's how men are: They try to hide their frailty, and that makes them even weaker. Do you think I agreed when they decided to kill me?"

Ay-Bebek struggled to recall the terrible legend: "If you hadn't told these troops everything you knew in exchange for that ruby necklace, they wouldn't be pouring over here! How can we save ourselves now?"

Aypi reared up like a trodden viper and hissed, "Woman, don't talk unless you know what you're talking about! They aren't enemies; they're my friends. They've come to take my revenge. They have no business with the village; they've only come to catch your husband! They'll take my revenge against men!"

Ay-Bebek swayed, as though her heart had burst.

"Come on then, let's tell him, he can get away quickly, he'll go out to sea and hide!"

Aypi cackled ruthlessly.

"Ha, do you think it's possible to hide from so many? These will find him, even if he goes to the ends of the earth. There's no safe place!"

As she said this, she waved a rag to the clanging throng of men shaking the ground with their footsteps.

"Come on! Here I am!" she shouted, her red spotted kerchief blowing in the wind. "Come, let me show you where he's hidden! He won't escape! His punishment is written, take my revenge on him!"

Ay-Bebek, horrified, felt a sudden surge of strength in her limbs and, springing from the ground, came at Aypi from behind.

"Be quiet, shut up! Don't tell them where Araz is; please don't denounce him! They'll kill him, they're our enemies!"

Aypi spun round and grabbed her.

"Those you call enemies gave me a ruby necklace, and those you call friends drowned me in the sea!"

"If they did, it was your own fault! Wasn't the first crooked step your own? You couldn't control your own greed!"

Aypi's breathing slowed and her face became white, until it seemed flame and sparks would fly from her mouth.

"If I choose to live well and have pretty things to decorate myself with, it's no one's business!"

A ruse occurred to Ay-Bebek: "She's a materialist, so unless I can bring this bitch around with a few bribes, she'll send these soldiers to Araz, it will be a disaster…"

"Aypi dear, please don't do this, don't destroy my home. I'll give whatever you ask, I have a lot of things; my chest is full of gold and silver. I have a silver medallion as big as a shield, it's yours, it's gilded too – and has carnelians! I have a seven-piece bracelet, that's yours too, just get rid of these raiders, send them away, don't kill Araz! Our children are so little, if you take Araz, I won't be able to survive. There's no one alive to help me, everyone's hands are full, and I've never lived alone before! How can you do this? If you take my husband, I'll die filthy, and my little children will have to beg at the doors of strangers! Please don't, Aypi!"

A covetous fire played in Aypi's beautiful hussy eyes.

"You wouldn't lie?"

"How could I lie?" sobbed Ay-Bebek, "and why should I? I gave my promise, and I'll hand over what I said, more even. I have tons of other things, they're all yours, but get rid of the warriors, send them back! Look, they're coming, if they get here, there's no saving us!"

Aypi twisted like a snake again, mocking Ay-Bebek:

"No! I don't believe a word of it! It's clear you're no royalty, what are you doing with so much treasure?"

The enemy troops crested the last dune, weapons glittering, and came streaming forward. Some of them, spotting Ay-Bebek, hurried their march, while some even broke into a run. Ay-Bebek now feared for her own life, besides that of her children and husband. She tore the silver collar from her throat and put it into Aypi's hand.

"There, take it! Take that for now, then I'll give you all the rest myself, if you'll just send them away!"

Aypi took the shining, gilded collar in her fingers, turning it round and scrutinizing it until all thoughts of the oncoming army left her mind.

"This's really yours?" she asked again.

Ay-Bebek was furious. "No, I've brought stolen goods to you!" she jeered, unable to stop herself. "How could I get away with wearing a collar stolen from a neighbour in a village with five households? When I was a girl my mother had it specially crafted for me, as a gift – but what's it matter? First it's gone to me, now it's yours!"

Aypi hesitated a moment, staring indecisively at the oncoming army. Then her eyes caught on Ay-Bebek's earrings. "Give me your hoops too!"

Ay-Bebek removed them hastily and put them into Aypi's palm.

"Take them, just be quick!"

Aypi measured with her eye the distance from the battle line, and delayed again. Ay-Bebek, unable to tolerate any more of this, grabbed hold of her and shook with all her strength, screaming at the top of her lungs, "That's it! Call them off now! I told you to call them off! Stop the raiders, you whore! Stop them!"

Ay-Bebek woke to the sound of her own voice, keening in harmony with the baby's. Astoundingly, she had taken hold of the cradle with both hands and was rocking the baby back and forth, who had woken up terrified as a result. Actually, she herself was drenched in sweat. On top of that, milk had apparently spilled from her breast while she slept.

"Goodness, what a debacle!" she muttered, taking up the headscarf that had fallen, rubbing off her chest and putting a hand down her neckline to clean the milk. Then she recalled the worst moments of her nightmare, and froze... "Did I give my neckpiece to that miserable creature?" Then remembering more, she brought her hands up to her ears—to her hoops. To take hold of them made her feel a little better. "What a fool I was: it's dire bad luck to give up something to the dead in a dream. Damn me, why'd I do that? She had me so scared."

She snatched the baby into her embrace and stepped outside the house. There were dense clouds everywhere, but she guessed the place of the sun and took seven steps towards it. She spit three times over her shoulder.

"God, protect me from misfortune and worse! Stop the bad dream from coming true!" she entreated. "Tomorrow I'll rise with the sun; as soon as I see your face I'll make an offering and pray to you, dear God! Even now I don't know if you've set behind those clouds or not. Please God; accept this wretch's prayer. Oh, Araz, Araz..."

17

Today, Aypi flew once around the village and decided that nothing of interest remained, so she headed out into the desert. After a while, she turned toward the city. Since her people would move there soon, it was only fitting she see it.

A person's accomplishments often prove the opposite of their intentions. What goal had propelled Aypi from the sea bottom, if not to make herself known to, and take revenge on, the men who had once sanctioned her? She had done so, but the result brought her no joy, since her actions only hastened the obliteration of the village and drove the inhabitants away. How much or little was beside the point – her accomplishment was the reverse of her intention, so all that remained was to see the new place they'd obediently land in.

Soon she was flying along the avenues, where the rows of shops and the city-girls' outfits impressed her greatly. The fantastic, unfamiliar fabrics and tight-fitting patterns drew her eye: "These girls are dolled-up! Done up!" Most of the citizens looked like those strange foreigners she'd encountered in her own time, what could it mean? Had the descendants of those who'd punished Aypi for treating with foreigners become hopelessly intermingled with them? What cunning they had! Perhaps those who had destroyed Aypi hadn't been merely foolish, but envious?

As the ghost wandered the teeming streets, her eyes suddenly fell on a conveyance making its way east out of the city, back towards the village. Her feminine curiosity was aroused, and she resolved to ride in this remarkable rolling transport. Without hesitation, she chased after the speeding contraption. Before it had gotten far from the city, she appeared at the first crossroads before the shining automobile, garbed in the style of the city girls. She barely had raised her arm when it came to a screeching halt before her.

"Hop in, beautiful girl!" said a dapper young man with meticulously styled hair, as he leaned over to open the passenger door.

"I'm a married woman, not a girl!" said Aypi pointedly.

"Even better!" said the driver, leering at his passenger's doll-like torso. "You're beautiful," he teased.

"I know," she answered.

"You're dressed very well too," he added.

"I know that too."

"Your eyes pass right through me!"

"How else should it be?" the woman answered evasively.

Looking at the desert road ahead, the young man asked incredulously, "So you know everything then?"

"I knew it all ages ago," she responded coldly.

"Is there anything you don't know?" asked the boy, paying no attention to the meaning of her statement.

"How is a woman better than a girl?" she asked, locking eyes with him, "I'm unaware."

"Before I married, I looked at girls," joked the driver, "Now wives look hotter to me." An easy grin. "That necklace of yours is as beautiful as a girl by itself, seriously though."

"Really?" answered Aypi, her cheeks flushing pink just like a living woman's.

Seeing the effect even this tame flirtation had on her, the driver was inflamed. "Some peasant who just learned to dress," he thought to himself. "I should've known from the tacky old necklace she's picked out of grandma's hope chest. Well, I'm the one who wins. 'What God gives to his servant, he puts before him on the road.'"

"Where did you get such a beautiful thing?" he asked. "It really catches your eye."

"'Where did you get that', they ask the thief! This is my own doomsday present. I haven't had it off my neck for a hundred years."

"Hahaha! Like I always say, 'It's been there for a hundred years! If you haven't seen it, open your eyes!' Speaking of which, don't I know you? If you're from our village, I must. What's your name?"

"You wouldn't," she answered, innocently. "It's been centuries since I've been around here."

He hit the gas, his laugh filling the air-conditioned cabin.

"Now look here, our personalities are so similar. There's a deep connection I sense. For example, you've just used my favourite saying.

Her cheeks flushed again, this time with annoyance.

"No, I am not using anything. I just call everything by its right name."

The driver solemnly adjusted his necktie. "Okay, that's fine. You're not the kind to put too a high price on your own beauty, but allow me. I bow before your delicate loveliness!" As he clasped his hands, then kissed his fingertips, Aypi regretted that she was no longer living: There were still men who could honour a woman's beauty after all! The young man continued, unaware of his passenger's thoughts. "What elegant fingers! Ah, but your hands are just a little cold, has the AC gotten too chilly for you? This is a Volvo, it takes a hundred years to figure it out!" he laughed. "Perhaps we should stop a while and warm our bodies? And what about this: Turkmen seven star cognac, bless it all! To our future co-operation!" He leaned avidly over her, pulling out a bottle of pink liquid from the compartment in front of her. Would you mind grabbing a pair of those glasses and balancing them on your knee?"

"What in the world is this?" she asked.

The driver thought it must be sarcasm, or at least a joke, and looked at her from the corner of his eye. No, she was absolutely serious; she didn't know what cognac was. If it came to good luck, when it rained it poured: a real peasant, she'd probably swoon right as he grabbed her round the waist.

"Let me stop the car here," said the bold youngster, hitting the brakes and pulling over into a hollow between two dunes where the flowers and grasses had already withered from the sun's fervour. "Wonderful! There's nobody else here but us two," he began discreetly, "now we can forget our troubles and relax; that means you too. I think there's something on your mind. Is it just a woman's fear of the unknown? Don't worry a bit. I'd never harm you; in fact, I'll be your hidden friend for life. Allow me to introduce myself, the name's Kerem, they call me Kerry in the city; I'm Mered Badaly's son."

"I am aware," she answered curtly.

"What's the matter? You hear Mered Badaly's name and think I'll judge you? Don't worry, I'm not a prude; my father's prudishness is enough for one village, and that's why I went to the city and don't even come back unless I need to. This time I had no choice, the old man told me to come get him and show him his new place in the city, they have no reason to stay here anymore, he said. If I hadn't met you it would've been a wasted day, but now I know this is the best day of my life! The point is, I live in the present, not in the past like my dad. A true representative of modernity!" he laughed. "It's constant fun when you're with me!"

"Is there anything constant left about these people?" she muttered through her teeth.

"Raise the glass! The first drink is to our meeting! And let's not be so formal. How about a more casual relationship, okay?"

"If you think so," she said, and brought the mysterious glass of pink liquid to her nose. The persistent, complex smell of the reserve Turkmen cognac, which would have invigorated a connoisseur, made the woman with the ancient necklace nearly gag.

"The window! Open the window!"

"Well, well!" he laughed. "Don't just throw it onto the sand, it'll only throw up a bunch of dust!" With that excuse, he nimbly caught hold of her hand holding the glass. "Look, take a little sip of it like this… first touch it to your lips a bit, then take a mouthful, and gently swallow it down your throat… careful… easy now…"

"My goodness! Sir, you are quite a paragon!" said the woman, her eyes flashing. "As though you've given drinking lessons to some new woman each day! You think you're so trustworthy that you need show no restraint around unfamiliar womenfolk!"

"First of all," the city boy said with mock outrage, shifting even closer to her, "don't call me sir, we're already friends actually. Secondly, don't be shy, there's not a living soul around except for you and me. Be yourself and relax!

"Don't say 'besides you and me.' Say, 'besides me'," warned Aypi.

"What?" he asked, astonished. "Aren't you a person too? In our society women have equal rights, and they're just as honoured and empowered; don't be shy."

"So we're equal, are we?"

"Yep, equal, don't hesitate at all!"

"So when they feel like trampling on it, men will bring women's honour down to their own level, is that it?"

"No, it's not like that, don't twist my words!"

"Well then," she asked, "what is it like?"

The boy saw the discussion veering in an unnecessary direction, so he snatched pre-emptively at the young woman's waist. He immediately drew his fingers back like they'd been scalded.

"Your body…" he stuttered, staring in confusion, "it's so flimsy, like… just like you're – bodiless?"

Aypi glowered "All you need from a woman is her body?" she asked bitterly. "Just a twitching body?"

"I need a lot of things from a woman, the body is just the nicest of them."

"They say your new bride is from the city," she said, trying to shame him, and at the same time indicate that she was aware not only of events in the village, but also the thoughts in his head. "Doesn't she have a body? When you have a city girl like that, what do you need from a 'peasant' like me?"

The fellow's fevered brain missed the significance of this remark.

"I married a city girl for the city and to have a wife – that's something else. You could call me an unmarried married man – a bachelor with a wife. My place, my work, and my fun are in the city. What," he sighed wistfully, "can I say to you? It's too complicated for you to understand, it's too subtle."

"What is there not to understand?" she sneered, her eyes filling with menace. "I understand quite a lot now, and you're teaching me the rest. I can see life around us; I'm not blind."

The ghost got out of the car, but to avoid alarming the boy too soon, she left behind an excuse. "Relax, let me take a look around. If someone suddenly saw us, now for instance, it would be bad for us both, whatever the time or the era. Once, these people were so principled!"

She walked over the dune and out of sight.

18

Aypi vanished behind the dune, then flew up into the sky. She hovered for a moment, listening and looking down on the desert and the world, with its thousand dreams and commotions, before returning to the youth's side. Just as though nothing had happened, she resumed the discussion.

"You know, I used to be a sacrifice to naivety. Now though, there's nothing hidden from me in the whole world, I can see it all. May I say what it is you men need?"

"Uh… fine," he muttered.

"Here's how it is: You men thirst for absolute control. So you need, as you'll see, some peculiar, fussy, beautiful little wife to defile – mouthless and voiceless, like a trained dog standing on its hind legs before you! If it's not true, tell me! When you didn't find its ilk here, you became anxious -no, not anxious, but truly panicked and exasperated! So you went hunting for a wife in the city, the desert, the jungle! Some of your friends have brought wives from across the sea, haven't they? You men aren't looking for wives, but concubines. When you don't find them here, you won't stint to bring them from anywhere else on earth."

The young man, somewhat stupefied by the cognac, resisted jocularly.

"No, my friends aren't looking for concubines anywhere. They find love! What difference does it make if they're foreign, aren't they women too? Don't they have a right to marry and be happy? My friends go off and when they see a woman they want, they love her and return with her."

Aypi decided to show him that there were few secrets still unrevealed:

"Put that fairy-tale out to pasture! What do love and emotions have to do with going from country to country looking for some particular woman? That's just commodity trading! If you find the necessary commodity, you buy it. If you bring some trafficked wife from beyond the ocean, then what? Where can you find some woman who does just as she's told, and not stay true to herself? Will you quest in the Amazon jungle for some brute who'll trade her honour for luxury? It's all because you're gutless and lack self-confidence! That's why you're looking for a deaf-dumb woman!"

"Lies!" shouted Kerem. My friends are individuals, and they can marry foreign women if they want!"

"There's no shortage of women here either, for a determined man!" laughed Aypi, after clapping her hands. "I've only lived a short time in this world, but I've realized one truth: The thing men most fear is independent females. You want dependent wives. This priceless ruby necklace once frightened men into murder, so they, wrapping it up in pretty words, took revenge on me."

Kerem hiccupped. "She imagines that awful knick-knack on her neck is worth something," he thought to himself. "She has no idea the amount of money that's circulating in today's world." Outwardly though, he took a different approach:

"Your necklace is an international treasure, it's not even a matter of price – it enhances even your beauty. Any man who lays eyes on it would become a pilgrim in your wake!"

"And if I took advantage of that," she asked ironically, "and cast off this country, what then? Girls can be individuals too; can't they find husbands from other nations for themselves?"

"Them? They're sluts!" he shouted breathlessly, without

a trace of his former tact. "If they're so motivated, there's no shortage of men right here!"

"Ah-ha! Is that how it is? If you bring foreign wives here, that's self-determination, but if a woman marries a foreigner, she's a slut! What hypocritical creatures you are! Our women and girls are sick of it! You can't even make them feel like real women, you mama's boys. Do you think they won't go looking for real men?"

"They're chopping down our nation and taking an axe to the root of our race!"

"No," responded Aypi calmly, "you're the ones taking an axe to the root. Our women are victims of your spineless behaviour!"

"You're wrong!" objected Kerem, in near bewilderment. "We're not spineless, we do whatever we want: Last month my friend brought a 47-kilogram wife from abroad!"

Aypi spluttered, and if she had had living breath, it would have caught in her throat, even without that sip of cognac. Then, taking hold of herself, she barked, "What sort of nonsense is this? Now you're trading them by the kilo, you degenerate?"

Kerem answered smugly, without batting an eyelid. "This world is one big market. My buddy needed a 47-kilo wife. So what did he do? He contacted a company he knew of, and they sent him a wife from Thailand of exactly that size. Don't think he bought her unseen! First he picked out her picture and became so obsessed that he couldn't live without her. He transferred the necessary sum to this company, and secured his happiness! The product arrived at the specified time."

"And what if she gains weight?" rasped Aypi, unable to restrain herself. "Is she not allowed to eat or drink?"

"She won't gain weight. The company guaranteed it; but if she does, he can exchange her at the seller's expense. This is really love, my friend is great at that: as soon as he seems 'em, he's in love! Her too."

Aypi could see that the degradation of women relied on the most refined methods in this age.

"Barbarians! Savages!" she whispered. "Where is the place you call Thailand?"

"The other end of Asia. In the olden times they used to call it Siam. How could I explain it to you... Have you ever heard of Mongolia? It's beyond that!"

"Why don't you just say Chin-Machin?!"

Kerem tried to do his best to explain, saying "No no, it's not Chin-Machin."

"What kind of country could be there besides Chin-Machin?! Afterwards it's just water! The end of the world in the east is Chin-Machin and in the west is Pereng, and everybody knows it!"

"All right, all right. But the world doesn't end in Iran."

"Of course not" said Aypi frowning. "The Earth ends in the south at Mount Kaf, at the other side of Hebeshistan. And in the north the world ends in Saklab!"

"I love your sense of humour, go on" said Kerem. He took a sip of cognac and continued recklessly. "So anyway, my pal doesn't degrade anyone. He just gets the product he requires. The reason for the whole thing is that he has an antique Louis XIV style Marquetry bed, made by Boulle himself! You can't imagine, cost as much as a villa. What sort of idiot would put any more weight than necessary on the thing? See, he weighs 103 kilos, and the most the bed can hold is 150 kilos. So he's got to find a wife that will fit the bed, right? And so he did, exactly 47 kilos!"

"Can you imagine anything more disgusting?" exploded Aypi. "If you'd just once put yourself in the shoes of these women! Where are their rights? Where's the humanity? It's so uncivilized!"

"Relax, baby-doll," said Kerem, "Your perspective is too soft-hearted for the modern world. It's… like your necklace. Is there anyone else who thinks like you? Everyone lives by their own rules. If you've got time, let me explain something."

"My time is your time," she lamented. "Have these mortals time enough for me?"

"Then listen. Another of my buddies also got himself a foreign woman. He had a business idea, and in order to implement it, he needed one more little cog – and he found it in the heart of Asia. Now his business is running fine, and I don't see anything wrong with that.

We live in a market economy, everything is exactly as Karl Marx said: *money-commodity-money!* But Karl Marx has made a mistake, if he had said *money-commodity-money love*, it would have been most appropriate! Then his theory would have worked forever; it would've become a total *perpetuum mobile*! To cut the story short, the woman whom my friend had brought over works hard day and night and is making a heap of money. He's got a Mercedes and she's got a Vespa. They're both satisfied – they both have achieved their childhood dream and what else does a person need?" he laughed merrily. "May it be ever so!"

"Your friend couldn't set this idea in motion himself?"

"No, he just had the idea," said this representative of the village's new generation, speaking as an economist. "Not the motivation for daily work. If you're going to open a restaurant that offers foreign cuisines and earn money that way, you have to act accordingly. If you aren't married, where are you gonna get cheap labour? True love creates the true motivation to work! Love is the greatest stimulant to labour!"

"So there wasn't a deserving woman to be found in this country?"

"This country's women talk too much!"

"Women are women everywhere. Won't the ones from other countries be just the same as the local variety after a few years here? What if they get just as demanding as our local women?"

"They'll need a lot time for that and by then either the prince will die or the pauper! One of my friends says that whenever his import wife begins to cry, he just hands her 1,000 manat and sends her into the city to spend it. So she wanders around, buys stuff and comes back happy. Unfortunately, we don't have any women like that left; ours need other things to make them happy. Endless demands tire men out."

"This isn't business, and it isn't love either," Aypi sighed. "It's just oppression of women, and pig headedness of men!"

"Hey, don't exaggerate! And you don't give enough credit to love! You know, my friends have smooth parquet floors in their houses and polished tableware. If you don't have a bubbling jacuzzi to warm yourself up as well, what's the use of an imported wife?"

"What does that stuff have to do with love?" asked Aypi incredulously.

"It's obvious you've been buried in the sand, when it comes to modern love! You get your import-wife on all-fours and on top of four dishes, and chase her around the floor! Have a great time! Then, you get the jacuzzi bubbling and dive into the bubbles where she'll nibble on your toes one by one, count them, love them – from one foot to the other! Ah, you're still too young to understand this sort of thing!"

"Oh, that's how it is?" asked Aypi through bloodless lips, her eyes flashing. "I can see what you need. Basically, someone who'll rear up on hind legs when you show them a fish, or sit happily before you like a pet dog; a cringing creature called a wife!"

Kerem ignored her displeasure. "Basically," he said, gravely repeating his word, "This world's all about gain! Otherwise, you'll be left behind and left hungry. It's not morality, religion, or culture that makes the world turn."

"Then what does?"

"Hey, you said you knew everything! But not this?"

"I don't! If you do, tell me!"

"Okay, in this world, profit is what really matters! Religion, culture, and even the morality that every age cloaks itself in are all just means to a gain! I don't know who first made up this rule, but we have inherited it from our fathers, who kneeled before the worst dictators ever in order to stay alive! They've instilled this mind-set in us, so it's not fair for them to be offended by anything we do now – I mean the ones that keep saying they're moral and we're immoral. That's total hypocrisy! What kind of morality is it, that's built on daily fear and lies? All this talk of morality is just a pretty skin to cover up coercion! As soon as it's removed from ideology, it dissolves into thin air."

"Sooner or later, you'll all be victims of your own injustice!" said Aypi, whose every word betrayed her increasing anger.

"Perhaps," said Kerem unconcernedly, "but don't let that put you out. I'm not the one who created injustice, it's how the world is made and no one else has any plan to fix it. When they try to chip away at injustice, they just end up making it worse. It's no different with us. For example, we were once a third world country, so the developed countries exploited us. Now we're a little wealthier and we ourselves can exploit the third world at our leisure. As you can see, the world is set up tier by tier. The strongest exploit us, and we exploit anyone weaker. What's so strange about this? It's like you've just arrived here from the Moon. You know a lot, but you understand nothing. You've got blinders on because of your strict morality. If you want, I'll try to explain it to you in simple terms: If men look for wives from across the seven seas, it's just their response to reality. In our times, the harmony between the sexes that nature designed has been messed up. Women've lost their natural personality, and men've become too submissive and they can't take it anymore. As a result, they're forced to look for the endangered tribe of natural women in dense jungles!" he said, laughing.

"Is that so? So what does it mean if a woman flees the country to look for a husband? Maybe they just want to live as simple women and with men who can take care of themselves? Is it the woman's fault that harmony between the sexes has been upset?"

"No, but the women were the first to disrupt it, and they'll be the ultimate victims. They'll never get husbands."

"'A stone with a hole in it," exclaimed Aypi, "never stays on the ground, there's always a boy to poke a stick through it!' Women will never have trouble finding men! It was men who broke the peace!"

"No, women!"

"Men!"

"Women blame everything on men," said Kerem, "but they're wrong, you know."

"Fine. Everyone's entitled to their opinion. So, you're also one of these men on a quest, right?"

Kerem found it difficult to give a straight answer to this. He took a sip of cognac and reflected for a moment. When he finally opened his mouth, the cognac had gone to his head.

"It must be strange to hear this from a newly married guy, but I won't lie to you. Yes, I'm looking. My wife is cosmopolitan and emascul– em– er, mensa– emancipated! That kind of woman isn't a normal woman. She's more like a supporter or partner: in bed, in childbearing, or professionally. Men though are looking for a real woman, even if she is from the jungle. Hey, come closer babydoll! Let me hold that little body of yours! Even if it's lighter than air, you're still the natural woman I want!"

"Stop fooling around!" she snapped.

"I'm not fooling around," slurred Kerem. "I'm telling you secrets I don't tell anyone else! I'm silent around my mom and dad, but when I'm with you, I babble. Why am I silent around my parents? I've got nothing in common with them. That's why," here the youth pinched his lips tightly together, "that's why my mouth will be shut when we get to the village, see? If I open my mouth my parents clutch at their hearts like they'll fall over, as if I'm the one causing all the world's problems. I'm just a man of my times, that's why I've a much better rapport with people my own age, not my parents."

"Why don't you defend your land like Araz?" asked Aypi, who had been wondering this for a while. "Why did you give up and move to the city? Isn't it better to be a native in your own village, than an outsider in the city?"

"You're totally wrong!" argued Kerem.

"What's wrong about it?"

"Whoever can't fend for themselves is an outsider! The one who can becomes a native anywhere. If you're poor, you'll be the outsider's outsider even in the land of your seven forefathers! It's hard to understand the modern world if you've got an outmoded mind-set. Anyway, what'd you say your name was?"

"If I say my name you'll get tongue-tied and lose your train of thought, so go ahead and call me 'babydoll' like you've been doing, maybe you can figure out the rest by guessing."

"Be still my heart!" said the youth, hearing this female double-speak. He grabbed the half emptied cognac bottle and filled up a glass. "You have a sip too, when winter comes it'll warm you from the damp."

"What can damp do to me?" said the woman, and she smiled bitterly. "It's all water under the bridge for me!"

"Damn, where was I? Oh, yeah, look at the women my friends have brought over: They were strangers when they arrived, but after they started working, they were no longer outsiders. Even the one I said was brought over to be the cog in a business plan isn't just any cog; she's this country's cog! So how can she be an outsider? Babydoll, you on the other hand, with this old fashioned thinking of yours, I just don't know…" He stretched out his arm toward the ghost's knee.

"Take back your hand!" she spat, rapping it soundly.

"Okay, I've got it… Some people take pictures, some take drugs, and some…take back their hand! But where was I? Right, in my opinion, if there's an outsider here, it's you, babydoll. You're clearly behind the times – it's obvious from every word you say and everything you do. You're the foreigner, and that's all there is to it. These women you call outsiders are closer to me than you are, because they know how to live life, but you, on the other hand, simply don't. That's why things are a lot tougher for you than for them. You know, there's only one real competition in this world, and that's the battle of the sexes.

See, war between religions, nations, and militaries will end someday, but the battle of the sexes is eternal!"

"Why?"

"If there's no battle of the sexes, life will stop; there'll be no progress, and no future generations! Geez, don't worry your head about these things, come on, let's have some fun! Just tell me babydoll, why're you so unsubstantial?"

"My substance," answered Aypi, staring coldly at the boy, "was sacrificed so men like you could lead your screw-off lives! Centuries ago! I've been lying at the bottom of the sea ever since."

His hair stood on end, and his laughter finally died. He asked with terrible apprehension, "Are you Aypi?"

"What's it to you?" Aypi answered sarcastically. "Answer for yourself, cur!" A white nightmare galloped towards them until, braying and rearing, it bridled up beside Aypi. "Get out of the car!" she commanded Kerem.

Easily mounting the horse in one breath, she brought the whip that had just materialized in her hand straight down on the luckless boy's head.

"You want some fun? Here's your fun! Enjoy!"

The boy fled, his arms over his head for protection, but how can someone on foot escape a mounted pursuer? No matter where he ran, the whip still played at his back and shoulders. The woman wearing the ruby necklace rode her white horse after him into the desert, lashing away until he was drenched in blood and sweat.

"Thank God I didn't run into this devil at sea!" thought Kerem to himself, as he madly fled from the whip's venom.

"Come on, scum! Take that!"

Finally, the boy's leg's buckled under the torture and he fell onto the sand. The woman gave up thrashing him, and rode to the top of a hill, where she surveyed the distance to town. When Kerem came to, in obedience to an imperious gesture from the rider on the horizon, he ran in the opposite direction, kicking up dust and going as fast he could to get back to the car and then the city.

Once the white rider was alone, she roared and spurred the horse on towards the village. These men had also killed her!

"Pah! I spit in your faces! Coward, who killed me in fright! If you'd had any real power you wouldn't have murdered me, but defended me instead! Men won't die from fear, or come to harm from a helpless woman! You turned my life to dust!"

She whipped her horse on as she drew near the town, and charged straight into the group of old men gathered for gossip in the late afternoon. They saw her only as a white whirlwind, but her horse's hoofs struck several of the old men square on the forehead, and they fell lifeless to the ground on the very spot.

Those left alive couldn't imagine what it all meant. "God in heaven," they lamented, "we've heard about black sandstorms taking people, but we've never seen a white whirlwind take them. Now we've seen that too. If a man lives long enough, he'll see every sort of thing!"

As she whirled back and forth through the village, she whispered harsh council into the ears of every man:

"If you need a wife, don't make her carry your own burdens, let her be a woman! If you hold your own ground, she'll hold hers too! But if you become women, what else can they do but become men? You've misunderstood everything! You even think that men choose women. What comedy! In truth, it's the opposite. God help the man disfavoured by a woman! Another mistake: They track their wives' every move, the wretches! Fools, don't you understand that a woman can deceive a man every step of the way, if she wants? What's so difficult about it? What's more, men think they're smarter than us. The rest of their transgressions are individual failings, and too many to count!"

Aypi reared her horse and shouted at the top of her lungs:

"So what then of these all-powerful men, they who think themselves the centre of earth and heaven?"

Her question went unanswered though, and her voice, just like a bird's feather, floated away with the wind and dissolved into nothing, while she and her white horse turned into a dissipating mist on the distant horizon. Way out there, where the sea meets the sky blue, the white clouds began to darken as the weather changed.

19

The islet had stood in the middle of the sea forever, just listening as the surf smashed into it. Waves big and small struck its foundations, boiling and frothy, then leapt up as if to fly away, but never managing to escape. When the waves did their worst to shake the island loose, it was almost lost among them, like a ship sailing without a destination. From its narrow side, Aypi's Peak did look just like a prow.

More than a few called the place Aypi's Island. The fishermen had never liked it. The far flung accumulation of merciless glittering anthracite and the vague associations of terror put dread in the hearts of all who landed there. When the FishPreserve inspectors were on his heels though, Araz often hid there.

Now he was in his refuge again and growing restless from sitting down too long. As the trim little FishPreserve cutter finally motored away from the island, he stood up from his cave in the rocks. Glancing around warily, he snuck over to Aypi's Peak. Standing at the very edge of the drop, he stared into the water. Just now the surface was at rest, and he could see down to the bottom. Araz looked at the mottled blue-green depths until his eyes grew tired.

As he turned away, he thought he saw something sparkle in the depths, just where that mysterious necklace from the legend was said to still be lying, and Araz shuddered. According to superstition, all who beheld it should expect an evil fate. Who from these parts hadn't heard the story?

Araz cast one more fearful glance into the depths where that accursed necklace rested, forever calling to misfortune, then turned and went back to his cave. There was an ache in the pit of his throat; from now on he wouldn't come back here – devil take the place!

A mechanical droning insisted on his attention: the FishPreserve cutter reappeared in the east and slowly sailed by. This time Araz could easily make out the raw young inspector scrutinizing the rocky isle as though he were passing it through a sieve. The pennant on the cutter's prow whipped back and forth in the headwind, like the flapping of a tethered gull.

Now the cutter buzzed around the island like one of those infuriating summer flies, one in no hurry to leave. Young as he was, the inspector had to know Araz's skiff couldn't outrun his own boat in the open sea, and must realize his prey was somewhere nearby – so there he was, circling the island. "Not such a rookie after all!" sighed Araz, grabbing up a large rock from close at hand, and flinging it with all his strength in the wake of the cutter. "Hoping to catch me?" he hissed, "I'm not here, I said, so that's that! Move along, or are you not gonna make your quota today?"

The cutter suddenly turned to face the open sea and began heading away from the island. Soon it was nothing but a black speck on the blue sea. "Could I get away before it comes back?" thought Araz. "Maybe I can."

He left his cover and began clambering down to his boat docked in a deep cove cut into the island, well hidden and invisible to strangers' eyes. The form of the cove was terrible, as if some eldritch leviathan from Noah's day had left an angry warning: "Not just you and yours, but we too, once lived in this world, and like you, we had teeth: Behold their power!" and so roaring, it had torn off a great slab of the island, then carried it down to the sea's end.

Araz reached the skiff ready to leave the hiding place, but the cutter, which he'd just seen shrink away, remained a disconcerting speck on the horizon. Now it was coming back again, so Araz reluctantly started back for his hiding place, muttering, "Whatever you say, he's still the greenest of the green! I guess you just don't want to go home. Fine then! See for yourself! Stick around…" he threatened the young inspector, "and wait for the storm!"

When he let slip the words, he hadn't yet noticed the changing weather, but he did now. If he'd had time to think about it, he would have supposed it to be the hereditary ability of those who made their living by the sea to sense an oncoming storm. In any case, he'd spoken the unspeakable, and he straightaway bit his tongue, glancing around apprehensively. His gaze lingered in the east, where an opaque, grey sky hung low.

The water was still calm and purring like a lazy cat, though shuddering and frothing a little. The bigger waves crashed into the island and broke up like shipwrecks, tossing up salty teardrop necklaces that glistened and played in the air.

A tiny kernel of panic grew in Araz, like some predator stealing soft-pawed up to his pulsing heart, and trying to carry it out again through his mouth. He shivered with unease.

He stared at the darkening horizon; though he couldn't see it well, Araz knew danger was brewing, and it would soon come his way.

A cool breeze blew over the water, but where was the pleasure in it, if it came from over there? The waves rushed onward as though pushed by some unhallowed force racing to the opposing coast coursing higher and higher. Yes, it was dire all right; conditions were changing by the moment. The horizon kept narrowing, and the weather moved purposefully, as if it were searching just for Aypi's Island.

The cutter cruised in from the southwest again at full throttle, and as it circled the island one last time, the officer on deck sprang up and yelled something or other through a megaphone. Alas, his words didn't reach Araz; in an instant the salt water doused and scattered them to the winds, entirely lost.

The inspectors headed towards the coast and soon vanished. Araz's sensitive ears could distinguish the receding sound of the engine amidst the growing sea rumble – it was gone for good this time. "Finally," he shouted with joy, "I thought you'd never leave!" though his reproach went unheeded.

Once again he ran down to the cove and his skiff. In haste he would slip and almost fall onto the black rocks, but each time, like a bat, pressing his whole body against the bluff face he'd remain upright. Instead, a skull-sized rock at his feet would go tumbling down to the jagged stone teeth at the water's edge.

When he reached the bottom, Araz tugged the skiff into the water and attached the motor, then dragged over the fuel canister he'd hidden. He filled up the motor's tank, and tossed the empty can to the bottom of the boat where big, gape-mouthed sturgeon lay with open mouths eating air.

Nowadays, it was forbidden by law to take sturgeon in these waters. The fishermen had gradually submitted to this, and stopped trolling for red sturgeon. Araz wasn't unaware that they were beginning to forget their own profession; After all, the skiffs and canoes were getting old, the tools were rusting away, the nets rotting and even making lures was difficult for most of them now. They had lost the accumulated experience of their ancestors and were now directing their abilities in new directions; seeing who could find work in the city and who could get farthest from the village. With time, the fishermen had adjusted to their new occupations and few now cared to go out to sea by themselves. If they did occasionally take their dinghies out, the biggest thing they caught was roach or herring. Since only a small number of men worked at the state-run fishery department, the earnings of the rest were tied to dry land.

Needless to say, the villagers didn't stop eating caviar, nor did anyone want to give up sturgeon pilaf: it was impossible to throw a party without it, but you didn't need to go out to sea to find it. After they'd put aside angling for themselves, they found other ways to obtain red sturgeon. The men from the fishery would get it cheap, bring it to the village, and sell it for a fine profit, so of course the village didn't go without fish. If you could grab up sturgeon for the price of herring, wouldn't you do the same? Sometimes they benefited from Araz's services as well. In short, even if they'd lost their traditional fish-catching ways, they didn't appear to be losing their traditional fish-eating ways.

Depending on the season, Araz would place either longlines of snoods, or small handmade drift nets. Today he had woken up at the crack of dawn to go and check his nets from the night before. Since it was Sunday, he hadn't expected to see the inspectors; the weather had been better than he dared dream, and the sea peaceful. He started to check the nets – a line of them running parallel to the coast – by following the floating corks. As he'd guessed, it was a good catch, and there would be plenty of caviar too. The spawning season of the sturgeon wasn't up yet, so if you had any luck, obviously you wouldn't miss caviar. Truly, the sea is the proper domain for a fisherman; what business does he have on land? Araz had been in a fine mood and he felt like humming a tune, and if he'd had time, he would have. Unfortunately, everything had gone sour when the unexpected but well-known FishPreserve cutter had appeared suddenly on the horizon.

At any rate, now the bad part was over, and he'd be able to return home uneventfully. At first he considered the gale lucky for chasing away the dogged, young inspector and was grateful. He didn't have time to take much pleasure in it though – there was trouble enough: He needed to get home quick before the winds came into their full strength. Ay-Bebek would be waiting, one eye on the road and one on the sea, worried as ever.

Araz started the engine and sped off from the island's east side headed to the coast. It was a pity he hadn't been able to check all the nets; who would have stopped him now? "Too bad about that," he consoled himself, "but I'll check them later," though as he well knew, after this storm it would be a miracle to find even the nets.

He covered a considerable distance with such thoughts, and the island's silhouette vanished behind him. Suddenly the tenor of the engine abruptly changed and fell silent. The boat kept on a little ways, but not far before it began to pitch and sway in the swell. The shore was still far away. He tried to restart the motor – nothing; and again – nothing. He continued to pull the cord to no avail.

The sparkplugs, he thought. He took them out, cleaned them, and put them back in place, but it was futile. His spirit trembled and, while he struggled with a powerful, metastasising panic, he took out and reassembled various parts of the motor. Wiping the sweat from his brow, he prayed to God, and yanked on the cord – but the machine made no sound. What to do? Grimacing, Araz turned to face into the wind. Just like a seven-headed, fire-breathing hydra from old tales, the storm front grew bigger and bigger. From some uncertain mnemonic wellspring, a terrible recollection came to him, and he pounced towards the jumbled, empty tank in the bottom of the boat. He unscrewed the cap and poured the dregs into his hand. He nearly swooned: On top of the filmy liquid in his palm rolled sweaty drops of water.

Then he seemed to remember seeing the children playing a few days ago and, if he wasn't mistaken, one of them had the tank, even the cap (God help him) in hand. The kids had filled the empty tank with water, no doubt about it. Araz, thinking it was filled with gas, had brought water out here instead. The real gas tank was probably arrogantly sticking its neck up in the shed right now. Enraged at his own deceitful tank, he threw it so forcefully that the skiff nearly capsized.

He sighed. It must've been the kids. Or somebody else? How to know? Only a few days ago, it now occurred to him, he'd been returning home late. As he had approached the house hadn't the receding back of an unknown person appeared for a moment in the darkness? He hadn't paid any attention then; people were always wandering by night and there was no keeping the young at home. Now he shook his head wistfully. Nothing was ever as simple as it seemed, was it?

He looked around uncertainly. For a moment he wavered, completely hopeless. Every moment was gold though, and he had to find a solution quickly. The black storm waved its giant, dark wings at him, and advanced. He grabbed the oars, fit them into their locks, and gathered all the strength of his arms to escape from the disaster bearing down on him. He began to row.

20

Clouds of downy pollen blown by the scorching wind landed on the hills and mixed with the sand, turning the entire area as grey as wolf pelt. It was hot beyond all endurance, and a bitter, heavy-smelling breeze blew from the sea. People found no relief: First they ran out of their simple homes, then they ran back inside. The old and the infirm had it worst of all. They tried to overcome the horrible searing heat by drinking tea and worried lest conditions grew even worse, but what was the use?

When the sun did its worst, the sand got so hot it began to stir and whirl over the hills, moving towards the sea. The searing dust twisted in the air as it blew over the village, down to the beach, and finally into the sea to temper the heat. The sea made its own depredations, sending water surging and boiling towards the houses, as it sought after a distant coolness only hinted at on the grey horizon.

In the afternoon, an oppressive silence settled over the coast. Earth and Heaven vibrated in expectation of uncertain danger. Creatures of all kinds retreated to their homes: bird to nest, beast to den. Only the gulls gathered up and flew low over the dark waters, squawking away to secret redoubts.

To the east and the west, where the battle between earth and sea was most pitched, grey cliffs drew back in trepidation as the sea mounted an offensive against them. The sea threw itself forward to escape from the scorching sun, head-butted the coast like a ram, and then retreated once more to recover strength from the replenishing depths until it could hit back even harder. At times, the water made inroads farther up the beach, scalding its extremities on the hot sand, hissing like a cobra. It would spit white froth as it rushed forward, then moan and draw back its amorphous fringes, licking wounds like an animal. A moment later, with that fervour of a cornered predator, it would throw itself towards the coast again.

At the high water mark, it seemed like the eternal conflict between land and sea might finally be resolved.

The sun didn't set, but drowned in the steaming, black mists, leaving behind it little hope of ever rising again. In its wake, the rumbling sky cracked open and dissolved into a swathe of black.

The villagers regarded these meteorological omens with dread. Old men with beards as white as their eyes sighed that they couldn't recall an equal calamity in all their days. "Tonight the sea'll certainly be *a guest*; there'll be no sleep, lest it catch us unawares."

As always, people thought of Aypi, and some even prophesied that the storm corresponded with the foreigners from the legend. As a result, the faded old tale received a new infusion of life, and people grew even more frightened.

"You've all found yourself something to be scared of tonight!" said fat Rejeb, scoffing at superstition, when the fishermen had all sheltered together in Hodja's fairly roomy house to pass the night. "In this era we've the power to punch a hole in the moon," but you're still aflutter about some tale from granddad's time!"

The feeble electric lighting had dimmed out earlier than usual today, so the men made do with a smoky, eye-stinging, oil-lamp they were now circled around. Rejeb's words disconcerted rather than comforted them.

"If you make a hole in the moon, youngster," said their host, who had given some thought to the moon's fate, "what if a poisoned wind comes blowing out of it? It's no good; to do it would be utter foolishness. If you go round doing these thoughtless things, wait and see; it'll just make life worse for people like us. That's why you, Rejeb, ought to make sure they don't! You're half city-man: a striped man on your way to the capital. When you get there, tell this to the scientists for us: Stop chasing after the moon and the sun! The cosmos has always been in the sky, so why meddle with 'em? Who knows what's on the dark side of the moon? No one does, and neither do we, so why should we delve into it for no reason? Have you already learned about everything there is on earth? If you get up there, who knows what could happen? You'll only know when it does, and by then it'll be too late! So there's nothing better than to leave those wonders be. Well boy, tell that to the scientists!"

The fishermen sitting by the lamp muttered accord with Hodja, and for a while they discussed outer space and argued about heavenly bodies. Meanwhile, the storm gathered force and shook the scattered houses until the men returned from space to more unavoidable, earthly concerns, such as their uncertain future. After this storm they might have to rebuild most of the homes, but where were the funds? It seemed like the folks relocating them would have their day soon, if there were no longer anything left to tie the locals here.

The children were becoming a nuisance, but the adults decided to stay put until the storm blew over. In the dreary, peculiar light, the older folk talked, while the kids sprawled at their feet watching the oil lamp's sad flame, which jumped and sputtered like a devil. The women stayed back, veiled in the darkness behind their husbands and commiserated in whispered ululations.

Hodja turned towards Gutly with a hope of giving people something else to think about: "Read those papers of Araz's, if you've got them. You had something with you when you came in, unless I imagined it."

"No, you weren't imagining it," said Gutly, picking up the thick envelope resting at his feet, and taking out a bunch of yellowed papers. "They're said to be from Araz's father's father. I took them to Ashgabat to be written out in modern letters; they were originally in Arabic letters– the old writing."

The audience began to pay a little attention. "Well, let's hear it then!" someone said.

Gutly put the old manuscript away and brought out several white sheets instead. "Let me read you some things about Aypi."

"In her childhood, no one spoke her true name, but referred to her merely as Aypi. When she misbehaved, her father was angry and he sometimes threatened: 'It seems the only work you do is breaking dishes: because of you, our home has neither a teapot, nor a cup, nor a pitcher! If you weren't my only daughter, I would have thrown you into the sea 'ere now.' In all the village, but one person used her true name, and that was her old grandmother. 'Why do you misuse your tongues? If you speak it, speak her full name: Not Aypi, but Ay-Peri! Is she some friendless orphan, that you abuse and shorten her name so?'"

"Few listened to the old woman though, and her grumblings did not change anyone's habits. After her grandmother died, Aypi's true name was entirely forgotten. Naughty as she was, this girl was quite skilled at swimming from a very young age. Once she stepped into the water, she swam like a fish! Besides, her beauty outshone most other girls'…"

Everyone was attentive now. "Well!" marvelled Hodja. "Who'd have guessed that our old legend'd turn out to be true?"

"It has a ring of truth," remarked Gutly, looking up from the paper. "But these writings seem to have been put down long after Aypi's era. It was a century later that old folks' talk began to be written down. Listen to this: "By order of the judges, as punishment Aypi was taken to an island in the middle of the sea, to be thrown into the water from a great height. Aypi, however, when she landed in the water, recovered herself and began to swim back to the village. Dadeli saw this, so he chased after her and held her under the water, though she struggled mightily. Yet, her strength was not the equal to a man's, and finally she had drowned.""

Just as Hodja anticipated, this part didn't cheer up anyone; instead, an even greater pall hung over the party. "Unjustly spilt blood doesn't rest, they say," admitted Hodja, as if to himself. "I don't suppose our ordeal now is totally unconnected to this."

"Are you saying Aypi has the power to take revenge on us?" asked Man-Weli.

The men all fell silent, including Hodja.

Unable to endure the storm any longer, the outer door flew open. The wet air, as though seeking out a particular person, flew to the far corner of the room, blowing out the oil lamp as it passed. Women gasped, and someone ran to close the door. Nur Tagan struck a match, and its dim light made the wrinkles on his distraught face, deeper even than during the day, seem like bands of pure black. The devil in the lamp leaped up to its dance again, and everyone resumed listening to the storm.

"We made fast all the skiffs and canoes earlier," said Nur Tagan warily. "That was a lucky thing. We should poke our heads out and check on them, in case *the guest* suddenly comes!"

The gale continued, though Hodja's house seemed barely able to endure, it creaked and shook so. The next gust of wind was poised to rip it from the ground and carry them all into the sky. They had to shout to be heard, as the wind wandered around the house whistling cacophony through every crack and crevice. The weak light of the lamp threatened to die again, which depressed everyone and reminded them how helpless living creatures really were before nature's arrayed powers. Suddenly, the tarp tied over the roof was whipping free in the wind, and the downpour had insinuated itself into the house. The men ran outside to set it right, returning soaked. Having tested their strength against the storm, their spirits revived a little, and they tried to jest with each other.

The darkness grew though, and their good spirits did not last long. Voices unconsciously grew hushed until the familiar solemnity held court. There was no telling how long this would continue. They felt as helpless as dried out stumps; in the sickly light between these walls they did look more like dried stumps than actual living people. The smallest children, exhausted from whining and crying, dozed off, while the slightly older ones, who still didn't know what a natural disaster was, couldn't understand why the adults didn't stop the unpleasantness, relight everything, and go outside. Yet older youngsters, proud as they were, tried to appear self-assured like the adults – at least in front of their mothers and sisters.

Not one of the adults ever closed their eyes; instead they kept listening to the sea gnawing at the coast like a hungry raptor, until the water's roar and the sky's thundering stopped for a heartbeat. It was just long enough to permit a woman's skin prickling cry to ring out from the very depths of wild darkness.

"Ara-a-a-a-az!"...

Everyone sprang up like cold water had hit them, then froze. Coming to their senses, they ran out into the storm and rain towards the sea.

The woman's voice echoed over the coast, like a chant to chase the storm away. With each repetition, more people came to the beach, and they seemed to hear the names, unspoken and forgotten for many a year, of all the fishermen who had never returned.

When they reached Ay-Bebek, she was as silent as the black stone she sat upon, and completely insensible. The wind tousled her hair, but she had roused the merciless night's pity. Now she sat listening compliantly to the crash of surf and thunder.

The fishermen were horrified when they realized that they had forgotten Kebe grandma too during the night, but they found her on the beach as well. The old woman looked like a wet cat, and shuddered with fever. They brought them inside, the old woman and Ay-Bebek alike. It broke the fishermen's hearts to see the stricken women looking like broken winged gulls separated from their flock. They weren't sure what their fault in the matter was, so they shrugged their shoulders in front of the sea and admitted that they knew nothing.

Their ordeal ended only with the return of daylight. The thunder, which had come to their very doors, slowly receded, and normal sounds took its place, until night and storm were gone. Everyone carefully emerged from their homes and went down to the beach.

The sea was losing its strength: it lay there gasping and frothing at the mouth as it clawed the coast like a purring, feral cat. When folk noticed that the weathered old ship was missing from its place, they all agreed, per the old superstition, that the sea had carried it home.

They chattered and tarried a while on the coast before dispersing to hearth and home as the sun climbed into the sky. Afterwards, without a whisper, they started to pack up their possessions and prepare to carry it all away.

Ay-Bebek was far from all such concerns, and she didn't spend a minute packing. As she always did, she went outside to watch the sea hum its old tune.

"We're staying. We won't move." These powerless words turned into a mute sob, and a tear came to her eye. "I couldn't go to the city and leave your father alone here."

Baljan came over with the little baby, who'd just begun to toddle around, and put the infant in his mother's arms. "Don't cry, mommy. Daddy's lost, but you're not alone. The baby and me are here next to you. Wherever we live, this is our beach. You know, the sea isn't moving – just us. Whenever we come back, the sea will be waiting for us here. It's our sea, right mom?"

Ay-Bebek considered this for a moment. "Yes," she replied, putting a hand on his shoulder. "This sea and this sky are ours. Just as love does, the sea honours loyalty. Whenever we return, it will be waiting."

Leo Tolstoy – Flight from Paradise

by Pavel Basinsky

Over a hundred years ago, something truly outrageous occurred at Yasnaya Polyana. Count Leo Tolstoy, a famous author aged eighty-two at the time, took off, destination unknown. Since then, the circumstances surrounding the writer's whereabouts during his final days and his eventual death have given rise to many myths and legends. In this book, popular Russian writer and reporter Pavel Basinsky delves into the archives and presents his interpretation of the situation prior to Leo Tolstoy's mysterious disappearance. Basinsky follows Leo Tolstoy throughout his life, right up to his final moments. Reconstructing the story from historical documents, he creates a visionary account of the events that led to the Tolstoys' family drama.

Flight from Paradise will be of particular interest to international researchers studying Leo Tolstoy's life and works, and is highly recommended to a broader audience worldwide.

Buy it > www.glagoslav.com

The Investigator

by Margarita Khemlin

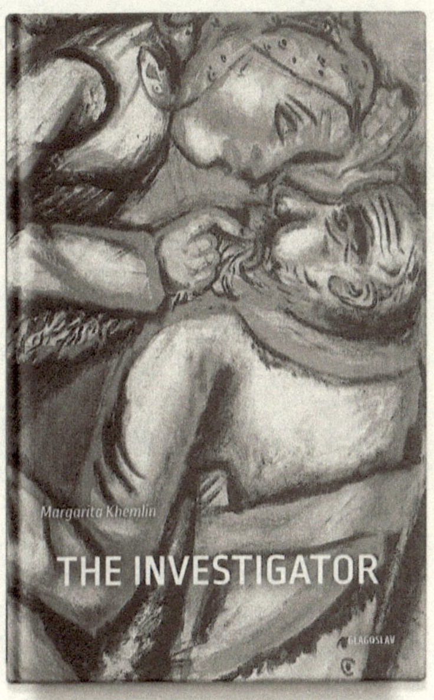

The Investigator is set in Soviet Ukraine in the early 1950s. With Stalin at the helm, the post-war Soviet Union is struggling to rebuild and to heal the nation of its multiple wounds. Plots and conspiracies abound and challenges to socialist values, real and imagined, proliferate.

A young woman is murdered in a typical Soviet town. In the spirit of the era everyone is a suspect. The investigator of the title sets out to solve the crime. A former intelligence officer who seeks to embody the ideals of the young Soviet Union, he introduces the reader to a polyphony of alternative voices that, together with his own, weave the unique fabric of this striking novel.

Buy it > www.glagoslav.com

Marina Tsvetaeva - The Essential Poetry

by Marina Tsvetaeva

Marina Tsvetaeva: The Essential Poetry includes translations by Michael M. Naydan and Slava I. Yastremski of lyric poetry from all of the great Modernist Russian poet Marina Tsvetaeva's published collections and from all periods of her life. It also includes a translation of two of Tsvetaeva's masterpieces in the genre of the long poem, "Poem of the End" and "Poem of the Mountain." The collection strives to present the best of Tsvetaeva's poetry in a single small volume and to provide a representative overview of Tsvetaeva's high art and the development of different poetic styles over the course of her creative lifetime. Also included in this volume are a guest introduction by eminent American poet Tess Gallagher, a translator's introduction and extensive endnotes.

Buy it > www.glagoslav.com